The Bridgewater Talespinners
present their
2018 Anthology

Spinning Tales
Around the Table

Riverhaven Books

www.RiverhavenBooks.com

Spinning Tales Around the Table **is an anthology of pieces – some true, some fictitious, some a bit of both. It includes poetry, short stories, flash fiction, memoir, and novel excerpts. Each piece is the heart and sole of its author. Names may be accurate or may have been changed, but the sentiment – the memories – have not.**

Published in the United States
by Riverhaven Books,
www.RiverhavenBooks.com

Printed in the United States of America
by Country Press, Lakeville, Massachusetts

Edited and designed by Stephanie Lynn Blackman
Whitman, Massachusetts

WE ARE THE TALESPINNERS

We Share Stories:

Stories about the mysteries, the follies, the absurd,
the personal chaos, the heartbreaking losses, and the
joys and passions of life.

ENJOY!

Ken Brack   Nancy Byron   Royann Charon
Adelene Ellenberg   Nancy Winroth Gay
Katheryn Marie Golden   Phyllis Goldfeder
T.J. Herlihy   Barry Kravitz
Velta Malvess   C. Quigley Muratore
Beverly Post   G. Anna Votruba

TABLE OF CONTENTS

SUMMER HOLIDAYS

It was summer – Everything was blooming, growing, and as far as the eye could see, everything seemed at peace. But our hearts were troubled and our minds, uneasy. Our country, Latvia, had already been through many frightening times. For many years we had lived under Russian communist terror. A life filled with degradation, lies, torture, and murder. For a normal, free human being, it is imposable to understand what that regime meant. Only those who have lived through it truly know how dreadful and evil it was.

When World War II started, ridiculous as it sounds, we were glad that the Germans, our most hated oppressors for hundreds of years, had come and driven the communists out of our country. Now, living under German occupation, there was no more terror, and we could sleep peacefully at night. We lived and worked as usual, but the rulers were German. Everything seemed fairly normal for most of us. However, there was one group of people living in terror – the Jews.

Under German rule, there were many restrictions. We could buy nothing without a special permit. Even food was rationed. Latvia, which was basically an agricultural country that had never experienced a shortage of food, suddenly needed food coupons. A single person living alone had a hard time getting enough to eat. Therefore many city dwellers had to depend on relatives who had farms in the country. Farmers lived under the same rules as urbanites, but they managed to have a little bit extra. The trouble was that travel was restricted. To leave the city limits by bus or train, one needed a permit, and those were hard to obtain. Lucky were those who had bicycles, for the road was theirs and they could go where ever they pleased.

I was one of the lucky ones. My parents had given me a bicycle after I had graduated from elementary school. Oh what a joy it was! Like growing wings! Little did I know how useful the bike would become during the war years.

My mother's distant relatives had a nice farm in the country where I had been sent every summer during school holidays since I was twelve years old. My doctor thought I needed some fresh air and some "fattening up" because at the end of each school year I always looked very thin and haggard. To go there by train these days would be extremely complicated, but I had my bike. I packed some clothes and off I went, free as a bird, singing and pedaling the kilometers away. When you are young, even a nice summer day can make you happy. There was hardly any traffic on the road. All the privately-owned cars had been confiscated for use by the German army and some of the higher ups. They mostly stayed in the city.

On the farm I tried to help with the work as much as I could. All help was greatly appreciated because most of the young men had been drafted into the army and sent to the front. We were an occupied country, and the Germans were not supposed to do that, but they did it anyway, and the Latvians were helpless to protest or refuse. Our farmer had two sons who had been drafted, leaving two others too young for the draft. The youngest, Karl, was still attending an agricultural high school and spent his summer holidays on the farm helping with the work. Karl and I were good friends. We had many things to talk about, many interests in common, and we discovered we both liked history, especially Latvian history. We realized there were many historical places nearby: some centuries old; some more recent. We longed to see them all, and one day we did just that. We took a day off from farm work, took our bicycles, and off we went.

The sun was just rising when we first got on the road. It was a bit chilly, but gradually it got warmer. It promised to be a beautiful day. After some kilometers went by, we stopped by the roadside to have our breakfast. We ate the sandwiches we had brought with us from home and then we realized we had brought nothing to drink. We stopped at the nearest farm and asked for a cup of water. Since the farmer's wife had just finished milking, she offered us milk, but we wanted only the cool, clear water to quench our thirst. Then we were on the road again, with so many places to go, so many places to see.

We came to realize we could not go to all of them in one day, so we picked a few. I wanted to see the centuries-old castle, Mount Tervete. Long ago there was a castle and a fort. A famous chief and commander who ruled the people tried to protect the country from intruding Germans. They eventually had to surrender. Nothing was left of the castle, not even the ruins. There was only a bare mount! One has to imagine how it once represented the strength, unity, and love of country.

We visited a big, modern T.B. sanatorium in a huge and beautiful park. My cousin had been a patient there once. Then we stopped at a little farm, "Spridise," which had belonged to our beloved writer, Anna Brigedere, whose stories, plays, and poems were loved by everybody, young and old. She had died some years before, but the farm had been kept in her memory as a museum. Karl was interested in seeing the garden and the black roses that were grown there, but we were not lucky enough to see them in full bloom. The buds were very dark.

Karl wanted to stop at his godparent s' farm just to say hello. At the time we arrived, they were having a mid-morning meal, and we were cordially invited to join the farmer and his household to partake of that which God had given. The table was set outside under a big tree and the meal consisted of typical, country, summer food – milk, gruel, boiled potatoes, cottage cheese, sour cream, and salted herring. We were hungry and ate heartily. This farm was very old, and the buildings still had thatched roofs. I was fascinated to be seeing something like this in real life. Usually they were seen only in museums. It was like history coming alive. We visited for a while, and then we were on the road again.

The road twisted through fields where ripening rye and wheat swayed gently in the summer breeze. Everything seemed at peace and I was glad to be part of God's creation. Chattering and laughing, we missed the turn we were supposed to take and arrived at the Latvian/Lithuanian border. The guardhouse was empty, and the barrier was raised, and no one was around. On the other side of the border was Zagere, Lithuania. We had heard of their outdoor market and all the things one could buy there. What could they sell in these times when everything was rationed and required coupons? It would be interesting to see, so we crossed the border.

There were shrines with crucifixes along the road, and we stopped at one to say a short prayer. There were also cemeteries that looked very old but were probably still in use. The nice, paved road ended and narrowed into a cobblestone street with houses on both sides. All this time we had not seen anybody – no human, nor animal. The houses seemed empty. There was no movement anywhere, but we had an odd feeling that we were being watched through the windows as we bumped slowly along the street. Finally we arrived at the marketplace. That, too, was completely deserted. We saw only a couple of birds enjoying a bath in a puddle. We did not know what to do, and there was no one to ask. Then we noticed a small hill behind the marketplace with trees and bushes around it. That must be a park, we figured, but where was the entrance, and where were the people?

Standing there confused and bewildered, we suddenly heard a voice behinds us. We turned and saw a very nervous, elderly man. Before we could ask him anything, he almost shouted at us, "Go back! I know that you came from across the border! Go back!

"Why?" asked Karl, "We wanted to see the park."

"You cannot go there. It is closed," the man replied. "The people are nervous and in an ugly mood. They do not want strangers around. They are hiding, and if you linger, who knows what will happen. Go back!"

That was all we needed to hear.

We jumped on our bikes and, ignoring the bumpy street, rode right on the sidewalk, peddling back to the border as fast as we could. Across the border, we stopped and glanced back to make sure the silent houses were not chasing us. We looked at each other, but we had nothing to say.

Silently, we found the side road we had previously missed and turned back to go home. On the way, we stopped at several other places, but the sunny joy of the day was gone. It seemed that a curtain of gloom surrounded us. It was almost dark when we arrived back at our farm. We went right to bed. Tomorrow would be another working day. Tired as I was, it took me a long time to fall asleep.

ALMOST AN ACCIDENT

The Second World War was nearing the end, but before that happened, my people were forced to leave their country, Latvia, and go to Germany to escape the Russian communist hordes. We had spent a whole year under Russian occupation, suffering all the terrors, humiliation, lies, and murders that resulted, until they were driven out by the Germans. Life was a little easier under them, but the Russians were returning, and knowing full well what would happen, we ran for our dear lives. If we stayed, we would be either sent to Siberian slave camps or be arrested to be put in prison and tortured. That was to become the fate of most of those who stayed behind. There was not a family that had not been touched by Russian atrocities.

So we were shipped to Germany and were subsequently relocated in several different places. The Russians by then were invading Germany and were right on our heels. My family had a brief stay in the city of Chemitz. It was a pleasant, commercial city, prosperous with sturdy old buildings.

Not long after arriving there, we were bombed out by American planes in their nightly raids. Buildings were exploding and the whole city seemed to be in flames. The fine old houses lay in shambles, their thick walls scattered around like wood chips. All that was left of the city as far as the eye could see were the chimneys. We lost some of our meager belongings we had been able to bring with us from home. The Russians were advancing.

We were put on the train again. All those who were not permanent residents had to leave because there were not enough houses left to live in. The train was long and filled with people. There were only two Latvian families: my parents and me and a young man with his parents. The others, mostly women with children, were refugees from other parts of Germany already occupied by the Russians. Their husbands were all fighting at the front.

Rumors were that our destination would be the south of Germany, probably the mountains, but when the train passed the city of Augsburg, it began to stop in little country town stations. Certain groups of people were ordered to get out of the coaches at certain stations. Finally, our turn came. We took our belongings and stepped out. In the station courtyard were men, with wagons pulled by oxen, waiting to distribute us to surrounding villages. Northern Germans among us were also foreigners because the southern Germans were completely different in their habits and language. One could hardly understand their dialect. It took a while to get used to it. The two Latvian families and some of the German mothers with their children were placed in a village called Lindach. The village consisted of one road running down the middle with five or six houses on each side. It was surrounded by their fields. The natives were not at all happy about the burden that was dumped in their laps, but they had to make room for us. The Latvian families were favored because we were adults. Nobody wanted the mothers with children.

Now we were in peaceful surroundings, but we were warned that the American spitfire planes were operating around the railway stations and big roads. Our little village was far from all that, so we felt safe and at peace.

My trouble was shoes. I was in bad need of shoes because mine were about to fall apart. I had lost my other pair in the Chemitz bombing. My father went to see the Burgomaster and explained my problem. At first he didn't want to hear anything about it, but finally he relented and gave him the coupons for a pair of shoes. In our village there were no stores, so I had to go to a bigger village that had a store. It was not far, I was told, but to get there, I had to go through a stretch of woods. They said it would be safe.

One sunny April afternoon, I decided to go to the shoe store. My Latvian friend insisted on coming with me. It was a pleasant walk through the woods, and we chatted and laughed, feeling as gay as the spring day. We came out of the wood on a little country road. Everything looked so sunny and peaceful. There was a farmer with two oxen plowing his field, and a little farther on, we were able to see the village.

Suddenly we noticed the farmer had stopped plowing and had crawled under the oxen's bellies. It looked very funny and we laughed. In the same moment we noticed a small object in the sky – a spitfire! It was not supposed to be here. There was no big road or railroad around. Nevertheless, it came at us with the speed of lightning! We were its target! My friend crouched down beside the road and ordered me to do the same. I was petrified: I could not move. I stood there frozen, my face turned up to the sky. It dawned on me how blue and beautiful the sky was, and how beautiful in it was the graceful little aircraft with the red tail – graceful but deadly. The plane started to dive to get closer to us, and I knew that in the next moment I would be dead – shot full of holes.

My mind was blank, but my heart was crying for God to help me. In that instant, another spitfire appeared, and in its haste to get us, almost collided with the first one. In order to avoid collision, both planes had to change course. Instantly my friend was on his feet. He grabbed my hand, pulling me to the bend in the road where there were some clumps of bushes. We hid there until the spitfires flew away.

Before I was frozen: now I was limp and could not stand on my feet. I had to lie down. Slowly, my hazy mind realized what had happened, and I shook with fear. I did not dare to leave the bushes, and I sat there a long, long time. Finally, we went to the village. There is no doubt in my mind that I am here only by the Grace of God!

A MIRACLE

It was the year 1945, and World War II had just ended – no more air raids, no more bombarding, no more running and hiding. Soldiers could return home and become civilians; people could start to live normal lives. But there was one group of people who had nowhere to go. Those people who had fled their countries still occupied by Russia could not return there – it would mean certain death. The American occupational army solved this problem by opening displaced persons camps, giving those unfortunate people shelter, food, and medical assistance. What the future would bring, nobody knew.

My parents and I were among those people. We had left our native Latvia and escaped to Germany to save ourselves from Communist atrocities, hoping to return when the war ended and Russia, with its communism, had been ordered back to its previous borders. Not even in our worst nightmare could we have imagined that the United States and Great Britain would decide to give half of Europe, including our beloved Latvia, to Russia! Everyone looked upon America as a symbol of freedom and regarded it with reverence. How could such a country have anything to do with murderers, communist Russia, who had killed millions of innocent people and force the rest to live under a reign of terror? Had they really understood what they were doing? One thing was clear to us: if we valued our lives, we could not go back to our native country until the regime changed or Russian occupation ended! I was very disappointed and bitter.

Our camp, Hohfeld, located in Augsburg, Germany, was occupied by three nationalities: Lithuanians, Latvians, and Estonians, each with their own section. We lived in blockhouses near a railroad-repair depot. In the beginning, there was a small section of Russian refugees who had escaped their own oppressors. Early one morning, the Americans surrounded that section and told the people to pack their belongings because they were going back home to Russia. No matter how much they begged and pleaded, there was no mercy – orders are orders. Some of them tried to commit suicide, some jumped out the windows. In the end, all of them were put into large army trucks and taken away.

The rest of us were tense and nervous. Was this going to happen to us too? What should we do? Where should we go? No use to ask the Germans; they hated us. In their misery at losing the war, they blamed us for everything. So we had to stay put and see what would happen. The Americans made an effort to persuade us to return home. But we refused to go back and live under Russian terrorism.

Slowly, we started to relax, and life went on as before. Many people worked in the camp or in a nearby hospital; others in IRO headquarters or the motor pool. I worked in the motor pool as a clerk/typist. I was also under a doctor's care. As far back as I could remember, I had had health problems. I was a very thin, frail child. I was a finicky eater who caught cold frequently. Now and then I had some trouble with my lungs. According to the results of the doctor's examination when I entered high school, the old scars on my lungs were healed and calcified, but I had a new shadow, as big as an apple, on my left lung. I didn't feel sick, but my mother was worried. I survived the war and its many difficulties only to find, after a doctor's examination upon entering the D.P. camp, that the shadow was still there. I was given many calcium injections and received extra food to fatten me up, but nothing helped, everything remained the same.

Years went by and people started to emigrate. Countries like Canada, America, and England, Australia, and others invited the displaced people to come there and start new lives. However they only wanted healthy people who could work and not become a burden. Old people and those with health problems like mine had no chance to go anywhere. In the meantime, I was growing tired of my monthly checkups. Every time I had to go behind the x-ray machine, I prayed, Please Lord, don't let the doctor see what is there. I do not feel sick. It's just a little scar.

Finally, in the spring of 1950, Dr. Stern decided to give me a vacation. She told me to enjoy the summer and come back in the fall.

She said that if I got a summons from the immigration, to go ahead and start the proceedings. I was to come to her right away, and she would give me a letter explaining my case. I told her that my father had applied for an affidavit to go to America, but I did not believe there was any chance for us. But she said we should keep trying and not lose hope. I did not know if I really wanted to go to America. I was still bitter.

Toward the end of summer, we were notified that our papers were in order and that we could start the proceeding toward emigration. Reluctantly I went back to Dr. Stern and told her the news. She led me into the x-ray room. She wanted to see if anything had changed before sending me upstairs to have x-ray pictures taken. As she started to view my lungs, she acted strange, pulling and pushing me this way and that, and asked me to stretch. Then she ordered me to go upstairs to have x-ray pictures taken and return in the morning. I was nervous. Why was the doctor acting so peculiar? Was my lung getting worse? I was fearful and did not know what to think. I was so worried, I hardly slept that night.

The next morning, Dr. Stern had me wait in her office while she studied the x-rays on the lighted screen. "Look at this," she pointed at the screen. The picture showed a nice pair of healthy lungs – no shadows, no old scars.

"It can't be mine," I said.

"Yes, it is yours. It is a miracle! How did you do it? Now, you can go and start your emigration process without fear. Nobody will say anything about your lungs."

I was flabbergasted. On my way home, still in a daze, I remembered my prayer. Please Lord; don't let the doctor see what is there. Was this cheating? I did not feel too comfortable.

A week later, we started the emigration procedure. Everything seemed to go well, but at the end of the day, I was called back to the x-ray department. My mind was uneasy. So it was cheating, and they had found me out! But all they wanted was another picture. I was so thin that the adult x-ray had not produced a good print, so I had to have one taken on the children's machine. Funny, I never had that trouble before.

Slowly I began to realize that God had given me a real miracle – a new pair of lungs! No matter how wrong it was for me to pray, or how bitter I was, He wanted me to come to America, or else why would He have given me the healing just before the emigration procedure? Whatever the Lord gives, the gift is perfect and lasts for a lifetime.

 **VELTA MALVESS** is ninety-three years old and entered the USA as a displaced person from Latvia in 1950. She worked in a hospital, an insurance agency, and did leather crafting. As a senior citizen, she does crafting, knitting, crocheting, and enjoys her love of creative writing.

IT'S TIME

"What's going on?" There was a loud knocking, grinding, and beeping coming from the basement. *What a racket!*

"I don't know. This is the third time I've tried to get the noise to stop. I tried to restart the thing, but this keeps happening. It won't spin out either."

My husband sounded exasperated. It was our washer. *Ugh, not again.*

We had named our front-load washing machine, Clothes Eater. Time and time again, it chose to chew, grind, and/or pull garments out of shape. Neither the washer instructions nor customer service were of help. Pushing the clothes back into the drum and using small loads hadn't worked. It was a crap shoot – I never knew what it would decide to destroy next. The warranty was long expired, too. Our appliance person shook his head with downcast eyes.

"Sometimes it just happens."

I decided the next time it eats one of my favorite shirts that would be its last. But this new malfunction was reason enough for me. We unplugged our hungry front loader for the last time.

I researched online and we went to the local appliance store. After having two front-load machines, the decision to go back to a top-load standby was easy, (Our first front load didn't eat clothes; it just broke down a lot).

A week later, our new appliance arrived, and it was beautiful. But when I saw all the buttons, I realized the panel resembled an alien robot. *Un oh, these cycles and options are nothing like my old washers. All I really need is hot, cold, normal, delicate, and the ON button. What had I gotten into?*

Feeling silly, I read the instructions on how to do a load of laundry. There were six steps to follow, and I was tired. I decided to try the next day, after a good night's sleep and some strong coffee.

The next morning I opened the manual and steeled myself to give it a try. Following Steps A-F in the instructions, I got my new washer going and sent up a cheer of success. *Yaaay, I did it!*

With the laundry washed, I was glad to get to the familiar part, putting it into the dryer. All was well. Then I got to the bottom of the washer or nearly. My struggle began. On my tippy toes I stretched like crazy but just could not REEEEEEACH the clothes on the bottom of my brand-new washer! After almost falling in headfirst, I stopped trying. Instead, I used my trusty step stool to help me get to the last of the wet clothes still clinging to the bottom of the shiny new tub.

I think the instruction manual should have a warning for user height requirements. But, for now, I'm considering writing the manufacturer to advise them that, at the very least, they should offer me a free step stool.

MY DANCE WITH THE PRAYING MANTIS

My husband called out to me, "Hey honey, come outside! There's a Praying Mantis out on the picnic table. Come out and see it."

I rushed out to see this rare creature. They are considered to be a boon in gardens as they eat bad bugs. I find them to be so interesting and exotic.

There he was on my picnic table. I stopped. The creature looked right at me. I advanced a few steps toward the table. He took a few steps forward as well. I moved to the right and so did he. When I moved to the left, he followed. I moved my head to one side and his eyes followed. His triangular-shaped head and almond eyes made him look like an alien. I moved again to the right and left and he followed again. Our dance continued as we walked around the table, first me, then him, and then back again. On and on we went. I didn't want to stop. Then the phone rang and I ran upstairs to answer it.

When I got back he was gone. Maybe he'll return again this summer to dance with me once more. My Mantis friend.

THE LETTER

The phone rang, breaking my concentration. It was a call from my youngest who wanted to share a few situations she was dealing with. I felt disheartened and distracted by the call, knowing I had done my best raising my family, as broken as my parenting tools were. But for now, I had to get back to the task at hand.

The spring cleaning was left undone for far too long. It was the bedroom that needed the most attention. After washing the windows, I started removing totes and a shoebox from under the bed so I could mop the village of dust bunnies living there. The box was stuffed with business envelopes which needed sorting. A fat envelope stuck out from the others and in it was a long-forgotten letter from my dad dated December 2001. I had to read it.

In it he explained he had forgotten to say something in our recent phone call. He wrote how much he appreciated the people my brother, sister, and I had become, each of us special in our own ways. He said he was proud of the volunteer work I had done for the church and the time I had given to help other mothers in need of support and that I was "the salt of the earth." I was taken aback and touched. My father had passed away in 2011 from Dementia. He left these words for me, knowing his lucid moments were fleeting.

My father had been so very tough on me growing up in our little family where no one ever spoke the words "I love you." Maybe this was his way of making amends. Or it was an "I love you" long forgotten. What led me to find it at this time when I needed to hear it? I want to believe it was his final gift to me, from beyond.

Thanks, Dad.

CURLS

At last, my much-awaited First Holy Communion arrived. But, my father was worried. He had no idea how to fix an eight-year old's hair or even get the right dress for my big day. My mother was still in Medfield State Hospital and couldn't help. I was surprised when he asked our next-door neighbor to lend her woman's touch. My father didn't know the woman the way my friends and I knew her.

Our neighbor, Aunt Mildred, lived next door with her husband, Uncle Oscar. My friends and I went over to visit them when their niece, our friend CeCe, came to stay on weekends. We adopted "Aunt" Mil, for short, and "Uncle" Oscar like they were family. Uncle Oscar was bald and round. A quiet man, he had a permanent red face due to his high blood pressure and squashed temper. They had no children of their own.

Aunt Mil was a small, thin person with a sour expression and a harsh personality. She was very particular about which rooms we entered while visiting. Her living room sofa was covered in plastic, and when she acquired a much-prized oriental rug with a white central design, she firmly told us, "Do not walk on the middle! Only walk on the red bordered edge!"

This seemed quite strange since visitors, on entering her mudroom, were slammed with the strong smell of wet dog. She kept her two Great Danes out there.

Sometimes CeCe's Uncle Oscar took us out for a ride in their small rowboat on Boston Harbor across the street. We enjoyed the boat ride, giggling all the way as we sat in the back. I didn't understand why he appeared so angry. CeCe later told me, "Uncle Oscar thought we were laughing at him."

But we weren't. *Why do grown- ups have to think mean things?* If I went over early on a Saturday she would ask me, "Did you finish your housework?"

I happily chirped, "Yup, I'm all done!"

"Well you probably didn't do a very good job."

The day before my special day, CeCe invited me to sleep over. Something wasn't quite right in that house. I could feel the tension and was afraid to move or say the wrong thing.

The next morning at the table, I watched as Aunt Mil made breakfast. I couldn't wait to enjoy the bacon she was making and the home fries, which were a new food to me. She put the bacon in a warm frying pan for a minute, flipped the flabby meat over for another minute, and then placed the greasy pork on our plates. All I could think was, *BUT IT's NOT DONE*, as I gingerly picked the raw onions out of my home fries. *Yuck*. My stomach was turning as I looked at the floppy bacon.

Aunt Mil caught my disgusted look. "What? You sure are a picky eater…. Hmff."

I hung my head in shame as I bit into my toast. *At least the toast is normal. They sure eat different here. Why doesn't she cook the food?*

Then it was time for my hair to be done up. Aunt Mil held a cigarette in one hand along with a glass of whiskey as she pondered the task before her, or any task for that matter. After a few belts, she swayed precariously over me for several long minutes and then began. As she washed and curled my hair, I was prey to her tough demeanor and condescending attitude.

"Hold still. Close your eyes. Sit up straight. You'd better appreciate this."

When she was done, I had the greatest banana curls ever and felt pretty when she held the mirror for me to see. I thanked her a lot for helping me. Then she sent me home with firm instructions.

"Don't spoil those curls and all my hard work before your special day. And don't ruin that dress or forget to return it."

Dad brought my mother home for the day to attend my Communion. After the ceremony at the Star of the Sea Church in Squantum, we went to visit my Godparents. Their daughter had her Communion the same day at St Williams Church in Dorchester. Always the camera bug, my father took pictures of her and me as we knelt with our hands in prayer, on the pedestal of the statue of the Virgin Mary. After the pictures were done, my parents, who were long-time friends with my Godparents, went across the street to visit with them.

Their daughter and I were playing in the churchyard when a small group of boys showed up. They had been watching us behind the fence in our pretty white dresses and fancy curls. Just for fun they teased us about our hair and frilly dresses and ran around the churchyard.

I have wondered about one of the boys who laughed at us in play. Could it have been my husband who lived only a block away and attended that church? Maybe by chance it was a peek into my future.

HELP

A few snowflakes fluttered down from threatening skies as I entered Mass that December morning. The storm, predicted for late afternoon, did not concern me. But leaving the church I tried not to be alarmed at seeing the intensity at which the snow was now falling. Nearly eight inches of heavy, cement-like slush covered my car and the parking lot.

I drove carefully onto the main road, hoping the plow had done its work, but I was disappointed. I drove slowly to keep steady as I approached a traffic light. When it turned red, I prayed, *God Help Me*! I carefully braked but the deep slop showed no mercy. My car slid sideways, spinning totally out of control. I felt as though this nightmare could take me home now. In what seemed like a nanosecond, the spinning stopped abruptly with a loud thud. Shaken, I dared to look. My whole driver's side door and roof were crushed-in. A utility pole stopped me. My driver's side window was shattered. Examining my arms, I tried moving them. My chest was painfully compressed and I could barely breath. Releasing my seatbelt, I was now able to breathe freely, despite the pain. My arms were unharmed. But I was still tightly wedged in by the crushed in roof and door.

Though my heavy parka cushioned the impact, the freezing air quickly enveloped me. My cell phone was buried in the console and I couldn't reach it.

Suddenly two men appeared at my window. I searched their faces, these two ordinary-looking strangers who took the time to stop, but I didn't recognize either one. They asked, "Do you need help?"

"Could you call 911 for me?"

"Anything else?" They showed no expression. My gut told me there was something different about them.

"Could you get my blanket in the rear of my car and wait until the EMTs show up?" *I was afraid to be left alone in the storm.* My teeth chattered from the cold and fear.

"Do you need anything else?" They seemed impatient, as the storm intensified.

At the hospital I was found to have internal bruising to my torso from the seatbelt, but no cuts to my face, despite the shattered window inches away. I had no side airbags; it was my seatbelt that saved me from more severe injury. My car was totaled. I asked the two men, their names before they left.

They said, "I'm James" and "I'm John."

As I thanked them, I couldn't help but smile and chuckle on hearing their biblical names. And they looked puzzled. Hmm…I mused, *Could they be angels sent in answer to my prayers?"*

A VOICE

Yikes! I felt my hubcap scrape the curb. It was All Souls Day and my mind was on the planned discussion for my weekly Bible study. I hurried in to my friend's house thinking, *"Ah well, I'll deal with it later."* After an insightful gathering, we stayed for tea and conversation.

My dark drive home was uneventful until I was startled by a voice out of nowhere. It sounded like it was coming from my radio. It said, "Georgeann, are you okay?" The woman addressed me by name and sounded urgent. I felt overwhelmed by an eerie feeling. She asked again, "Are you all right? Were you in an accident?"

I had goose bumps. *This was beyond creepy! Should I stop the car and run? Was this really happening?* My mind was in overdrive. *Had I gone mad?* Finally, my voice shaking, I blurted out, "Who ARE you?"

"This is Onstar. Are you okay?"

Whew! In that moment, I let out a sigh of relief. My hair-raising experience was over. It was not a prank or a haunting on this All Souls Day. Finally, my drive home became a peaceful one.

G. ANNA VOTRUBA began writing through journaling. As a local  Quilt Guild member she interviewed and wrote members' biographies for their newsletter. Anna is an accomplished multi-medium home crafter and painter who has made over two hundred quilts for family and charity. She is presently writing her memoir.

POET TUMBLED LOOSE

Her life was like a jail. She zippered shut her lips at teachers' misunderstandings, playground bullies, her stepfather's drunken rages. The written word kept her alive. Years later, her husband struck her down in front of their children. The children shrieked, hid in corners. She fought back but lost. He was twice her size. She muttered incantations till the day he went to jail. When her oldest was caught smoking weed, the judge sentenced jail-time. When her dog ran away, it was locked up in the city pound. Even her dog did time.

One day, she had enough. She pressed her spirit forward till the walls crumbled at her feet. She arched her neck like Queen Nefertiti, embraced her children, spoke words of power. As the truth tumbled loose, poetry bloomed from her lips like daily prayer. The day she became a poet, her life began anew.

WORD

I love
when Poetry jumps into the ring
    lands feet first
        a real contender
    dares to get REAL
        despite artifice and groomin'

I love
when Poetry brews raw energy an' meanin'
    outta a poet's
        empty hot air.

I love when a poet's tremblin' voice
    blows hot breath into Word
        windsails Word
makes Word writhe and dance and pray,
    just as God blew forth Life
        to animate Adam and Eve
        from clay.

I love when Word empowered
    makes irreverent faces
        chastises and heals,
    tells cautionary tales
        gives pokes and tickles.

I love when Word
    shakes loose them golden apples
        from fabled Wisdom Tree
          danglin' ambition-damnation
        just beyond

our graspin' reach.

I don't even mind much
    when Word humbles me
       with clarity
    and sheer   bodacious   audacity

like a riff
that rings true

    like the first time
  ya ever REALLY listened
    to John Coltrane
  and what he could say
    with just his horn

           BUT…

since we poets play Word
  insteada instruments
    an' we don't get ta do rock concerts

we gotta get REAL

from our internal
   an' very personal
spoken   Word   within

We apprentices of Word
  gotta gather up a roomful
of wordsmiths and word-gardeners

word-hunters and word-gatherers
word-jugglers and word-songers,
those folks
who still know how to treat Word
with some kinda respect.

We gotta gather up a roomful
ta slam some poetry together
ta see if it will chime
ta cast it out before our peers
ta see if it will shine
ta watch what happens wit'
our child wood blocks clappin'

Now watch how
blocks of Word towers gonna come
tumblin' down
as Joshua's gladful trumpets resound
Now watch how
gonna bring those mighty walls
of ancient Jericho
a'tumblin' down, a'tumblin' down

Now watch how

Humpty Dumpty ego's gonna get cracked
rhyme omelet's gonna get cooked
or was it gonna be your goose?

My goose?

Well, hey, now, ain't that just the blues juice?

Fellow wordsmith:
    even if it is
your goose being served up for supper tonight

don't you fret
don't you shrink away

you be bold   shine bright
dare to summon   your good cheer

poetry ain't for the feeble-hearted
poetry ain't for the narrow spirits
poetry ain't for the high and mighty
      crownin' themselves with laurels

Fellow Wordsmith:
    come rejoice with me
      in the slammin'
        of the mighty
WORD!

STEADFAST AND TRUE

Our goat sucks in mouthfuls of steaming-hot water, as if drinking a clear cup of tea. Water shivers in the rubber farm bucket as he slurps. Steam rises in the frigid air around his face. Outside of Boston, the snow is six feet high against my front door, and thigh-high across our broad, backyard acres. To tend to our barnyard animals, I am forced to plunge against the snowdrifts, carrying an armful of hay and their bucket of hot water. I sweat into layers of clothing, while icicles form on my scarf. Snow shimmers in the gloomy winter dusk.

Bodi, our goat, is excited by my approach. He rams his curved horns against the tree-like neck of our seated llama, Dillon. Dillon just blinks. Surely, those horns hurt him. Maybe not. Dillon's thick hair, which coats him like cinnamon-colored dreadlocks on his tall body, must have padded the blow. My family and I could have cut off – stolen – his hair from him. I could have woven a blanket for my family. Llamas are not shorn to the skin like sheep; we would have cut his hair to within four inches of his body. But we decided to let him wear his own blanket-to-be for these twenty years. He needs it more than we do here in New England.

Dillon has been with our family since our children were ten and five. Our children have led Dillon through county parades, town fairs, and 4-H Club events. Our children are grown now. My husband and I perform the chores, keeping fit.

‡ ‡ ‡

Sleepless, I leave our bed at 2 a.m. to trudge downstairs. I plop on a sofa-bed in our book-filled computer room. The sofa-bed hugs the wall; I press my nose to the chilly windowpane. I stare at our backyard corral and barn. The outdoors are lit up by a three-quarter moon. It is quiet, clear, and cold.

Behind our barn and corral are miles of deep forest. Land developers have coveted this land for years; their bulldozers would ravage the woods. But my husband and I, along with our neighbors, have thwarted the developers so far.

At 3 a.m., two deer appear. No doubt, they are lured by the scent of hay, piled high in the hayrack of the small, blue barn. They approach the corral's fence, noses pointed in delicate stance.

Dillon emerges from the barn. He guards the open door. Does he envy the deer their freedom, their lack of a fence? Bodi peeks out. He is uncharacteristically silent. Usually he "baaaahs" at both humans and animals or clashes his horns against the barn walls. By contrast, Dillon is a silent creature, with huge, long-lashed, soulful eyes.

Bodi's behavior curiously combines bravery and cowardice. He is brave against Dillon. Dillon treats Bodi like a rambunctious "kid" who is disrespectful to an indulgent grandfather. But Bodi scurries behind Dillon at the least bit of irregularity, as if he knows he would make a good meal for a hungry predator. Indeed there are coyotes roaming the skirts of the forest. And they are not alone in their hunger. Our friend from the West Indies has remarked on her fondness for goat stew. Just looking at Bodi makes her mouth water, she says.

Meanwhile, the llama, the goat, and the two wild deer are poised in a frozen landscape. A series of howls pierce the night.

The deer flee.

Dillon remains sturdy, unmoving, alert. Bodi scuttles deeper into the barn.

‡ ‡ ‡

A fellow "townie," who kept a dozen sheep on his land (but no llama), watched his herd be diminished, one by one, over several seasons. The worst part, he said, was finding yet another sheep carcass, throat torn out, blood pooling in black puddles, blood staining the tender fleece.

Out West, in North America, the sheep ranchers use llamas to guard their herds from wolves and coyotes. Llamas, ordinarily mild-mannered, are fierce protectors of their flocks. Dillon has a flock, now, of just one: the feckless, fearful, and greedy-for-hay Bodi.

Until recently, we also had Bodi's mother, making Dillon's flock a total of two goats. Before she came to us, she produced milk for a local dairy-goat farmer. The farmer established his dairy-goat farm to supply mothers whose babies were allergic to cows' milk. The first baby fed from his farm was his own daughter. But when Bodi's mother came to us, she was past being bred, past being milked. She retired to our barnyard menagerie.

‡ ‡ ‡

In twenty years, the only time we heard Dillon's voice, was the day Bodi's mother died. He howled and moaned when she collapsed in the corral. Frenzied, he tried to lift her back into a standing position by biting the back of her neck to raise her up. When she failed to stand, he began lightly kicking her with his front legs, as if to say, "Get up, get up!" My husband lassoed him and tied him to a nearby tree within the corral. Dillon was writhing against the rope and gnashing his teeth. I extricated Bodi's mother from the mud in which she was mired. She gallantly staggered forward to the water bucket and drank a bit. Dillon settled, slightly, but his huge, glistening eyes stilled rolled. The next day, Bodi's mother was dead in the barn, curled in a corner. We buried her deep in the woods. Dillon watched us from the corner of his eye. He knew.

‡ ‡ ‡

Guarding his flock-of-one gives Dillon a purpose. I notice elusive shadows slinking across the white purity of the snow. Dillon stands even taller and broader, ears pointed forward. I blink to clear my strained vision in the dim moonlight. Finally I see what has him on alert. Coyotes circle the corral. Dillon stands vigilant, a life-and-death drama unfolding in our own backyard.

The shadows slink and retreat, slink and re-group. My eyes burn. I must watch. Dillon is alert, still as a statue, conserving his energy. My eyes burn fiercely. It is 4 a.m. and they close against my will. I yield to rest my head against the nubby upholstery of the sofa-bed. There is nothing I can do. I cannot personally fight off the circling coyotes. It will be decided without me.

‡ ‡ ‡

It is 7 a.m. when I wake, stiff-necked and groggy. I scan the yard for clues. There is no trail of blood and flesh across the snow in our corral. I spot Dillon and Bodi eating hay that fell to the barn's doorway. Joy, oh, joy!

This afternoon, I will carry an armful of hay to refill their hayrack. I will haul buckets of steaming water through the thigh-high snow. I will watch an excitable Bodi gulp the hot water like therapeutic tea, warming his insides against the wind chill. And I will know that, due to Dillon's vigilance, death and destruction were averted. All will be well. Life is good. Our llama is steadfast and true.

THE GAMBLER

My ex-husband gambles on steamboats that ply the Mississippi River. He freaks out his fellow gamblers with a creepy black crow that perches on his left shoulder. Other gamblers suspect that the crow's dark spirit sucks their mojo dry and makes their tosses go sour.

My ex divorced me for red-haired arm candy. Did I deserve that, after I had borne him four children? So far, he's gone unpunished.

Yesterday he sat in the steamboat lounge, casually birdless, cleaning his teeth with a toothpick. His moccasin-shod feet stretched forward as he digested his meal.

His red-headed paramour chattered non-stop. He wasn't listening.

"That was a dish fit for a king!" announced my ex, after a belch.

As head chef on his favorite steamboat, now, I began to giggle.

His gambling ways...unbeknownst to him...gone.

Four and twenty blackbird-bits were baked in that pie.

IN THE MIDDLE YEARS

Long gone the dewy skin of youth,
the supple muscles with quick spring,
the bright gleam of sharp tooth,
the dreams of fortune taking wing.

Now it's time to pause and ponder,
calculate the gain and loss,
treat unknowns with sense of wonder,
as mysteries yet to cross.

Do souls run on electricity?
And why do spirits haunt this house?
What is it that makes you love me?
Must Good and Evil forever joust?

As I get older, my wonder grows,
while my certainties become bereft,
till I am left undone, Lord knows,
with only Faith to provide the rest.

MARY-MOSES SUPPOSES

Ethan's bringing home his new, pregnant wife, Arabella. I don't know what to make of a woman named Arabella. Will she be spoiled and flighty? Will she be beautiful, as her name implies? Ethan says not to judge people by their names because people can't help the names they've been given. But I think people tend to grow into the names bestowed upon them. Naming a baby is a heavy responsibility because it can be the basis of that child's character.

Ethan, my thirty-six-year-old son, is wickedly handsome and generally unemployed.

He's spent years trying to "make it" as an actor out in fickle Hollywood. Now he's heading home, wife and babe-to-be in tow. Hmph. I'm of two minds about it. Hope he's not coming home as a deadbeat, although I look forward to the arrival of a grandchild. Also, I like my solitude. I've been a widow since my Albert died of heart troubles. Albert's spirit visits me on summer evenings when I rest in my porch rocker under the stars. He twinkles at me, makes me smile.

Yet this change has stirred me up to redo part of this house for them. This Ohio farmhouse, built in 1835, slices into the side of a hill. The lowest level is the root cellar. Always cool in summer, warm in winter. Best of all, it's graced with an underground spring at one end. The sweetest water I've ever tasted.

I'm redoing the front of the cellar for Ethan, Arabella, and the baby. It's not as grim as it sounds. I'm not making them live in a hole in the ground. The front end opens onto big glass doors that face south, where the hill falls away. The golden sunshine slants onto the inner pine floor, and beyond the outer slate patio, the green lawn slopes down to a cluster of trees bent over the brook.

I've been busy scraping off this crazy-ugly pineapple-patterned paper from the original plaster walls. I decided to get off every last bit of this wallpaper, even though it meant I had to move the heavy hutch that leaned against the back wall. Imagine my surprise when I finally shoved the hutch aside and discovered a hidden door.

I was sweaty from shoving the hutch, so I gave an impatient shove to the door, thinking it was going to be a closet. Whoa! Hardly. It was a long room that extended deep into the hillside.

A rush of air met my face, smelling earthy, like moss and rainwater. My heart raced. I drew back and went to get a flashlight.

As I rummaged in a kitchen drawer, I debated with myself whether I really wanted to find out what was in the bowels of this old farmhouse. "If you don't find out, you will never forgive yourself," I said to myself. "Just go and do it."

Standing at the open doorway again, I aimed the flashlight beam into the depths. I stood still and listened for several long minutes but heard only silence. Gingerly, I lowered my left foot onto the stone step entry. The stone was smooth, well-worn, as if many feet had passed over it. I bent my neck to enter the gloomy chamber. The floor was packed dirt. Wooden beams supported the weight of the hill overhead.

As I moved the flashlight beam about, I saw wooden bunkbeds, built three-people-high. Tattered pillows and shreds of blankets were strewn across the bunks. The bunkbeds lined the sides of the low, long room. In the center of the room was a long, thin wooden table, flanked by a narrow bench on each side. As I raised my flashlight, I saw a solitary lantern hung from a beam. I was so curious, I approached the table.

There were tin plates, tin cups, spoons, and candle stubs left behind.

My curiosity drove me to go deeper into the gloom. At the far end of the table was a bundle of rags lying on the floor. I couldn't resist. I just had to poke the cloth bundle with a cautious finger. The cloth unfurled, revealing a pale bone that gleamed under the flashlight. With trepidation, I gave a poke to the bone. Was it a chicken bone? The skeleton of a cat? I couldn't stop myself. I had to see what it was. As I poked the rags a bit more, a ball of bone the size of a lemon rolled out. I aimed the flashlight right at it. Yikes! I saw a tiny, empty skull staring up at me. A baby's skull, it was so small.

Why was this unburied, abandoned baby here, in this underground cavern? I asked myself. In a flash, I knew. Of course! This was part of the "Underground Railroad."

This Ohio farmhouse, a mere forty miles north of the Ohio River, infamous barrier between free-soil Ohio and slave-owning Kentucky, had been a "Station" on the Underground Railroad.

Probably this very room was where a runaway slave woman had given birth to a child.

A child born too early, too small. No doubt the very earth that surrounded her during childbirth had muffled her cries of pain. She had no way to properly bury this child. So she had to wrap it in a shroud. Maybe she had other children in tow. She had to complete her journey to freedom.

I re-wrapped the skull and fragile skeleton in the rags, and placed it down on the dirt floor gently. My thoughts were whirling. I didn't know what to do.

‡ ‡ ‡

Two weeks went by. Finally, Ethan and Arabella arrived in their beat-up truck, stuffed with all their worldly goods. Arabella turned out to be a twenty-eight-year-old dark-haired beauty in the rosy bloom of first pregnancy. They looked vigorous and happy.

They weren't fazed by the long drive from LA, or the truck's blown gasket outside of Denver. They were blissfully in love.

I waited until they had settled in to let them know.

Ethan and Arabella were both fascinated by the secret room. I confessed that I was worried. Had my uncovering the baby's remains stirred up anything? Would there now be a "haunting" of this farmhouse?

Yet, I admitted, maybe my worries were unfounded. As acutely aware of the farmhouse's atmosphere as ever, I had not felt even a whisper of a presence. And I had certainly never felt anything amiss in the half a century I had lived here before.

Still, we decided to be cautious. To err on the side of Angels.

It was Arabella who suggested that we conduct a "naming" for the stillborn babe who had been left behind. A "naming" would tether the baby's soul to the Afterlife and help it move along its trajectory. It was best to appease the spirits, lest they become angry.

The task of settling upon a suitable name was not easy. I parked my bottom in my porch rocker and gazed up at the starry sky. I posed the question to my Albert – what name would he suggest? I swear to this day I heard his voice inside my head, telling me what I brought forth to the others: we didn't know if the babe had been male or female. The baby had probably been stillborn. Nevertheless, the babe had been born on "free-soil-Ohio" – and had made it to freedom against all the odds – so we named the child Moses. And because the child may have been female, we tacked Mary in front of it. So the child became Mary-Moses.

Mary-Moses supposes he/she made it to Freedom. Blessed Freedom. Lovely Freedom. Praise be.

After the "naming" Ethan announced that our Station on the Underground Railroad was going to be his new calling. He would be a tour guide of the premises. Even better, he was going to bottle and sell the water from our underground spring. Hmph. He may not be a deadbeat after all.

Arabella soon gave birth to my new grandson, Bolivar. Arabella claims Latin-American heritage and said Simon Bolivar is a South American freedom fighter. She said their son deserved a freedom-inspired name, also. My grandson is a delight, despite his outlandish name. I call him Bo. He and his parents have moved up to the second floor with me. What will be his destiny, with such a name, I wonder?

The cellar and outdoor patio are given over to the occasional visitor who pursues a passion for history and/or racial justice. We serve our visitors home-made cookies we call "Stars of Freedom."

On summer nights, I watch the multitudes of stars twinkling – the souls of all those who have passed, including those who fled enslavement on their way to the blessings of freedom. My Alfred is up there among them. It turns out we are never alone in this world. My smiling heart is open to endless possibilities.

THE SWEETNESS OF UNCONDITIONAL LOVE

Rona had been voted "most beautiful girl" in her N.Y. high school.

Her husband, Ed, was an ambitious accountant who was amazed he'd snared the beauty queen. Perry and Vita, also Manhattan-dwellers, had attended high school with our dinner-party hosts, as had Dale, my husband for all of two weeks.

Conversation swirled around life in Manhattan, off-Broadway shows, and art-gallery openings. Hailing from "fly-over country," I sipped my wine and listened.

Eventually, the talk turned to fashion and hair.

"My hair is styled by Andre at Vidal Sassoon's shop over on Fifth Avenue," said Rona. "He's so talented."

We gazed at Rona's perfectly-trimmed black hair that framed her large violet eyes. "He's a bargain at only $200.00."

"Pierre, at Vixen's, charges the same!" said Vita.

The New York ladies turned to me. "Where do you go to get your hair cut?"

"Me?" I muttered. I looked down at my plate. "I don't make a fuss."

Just then, Ed emerged from the kitchen, a striped apron over his crisp, white shirt. He stood aside, holding a flaming platter aloft.

The ladies' eyes remained on me, curious. "Okay," I confessed. "Dale cuts my hair."

Their eyes rolled in unison as Ed announced, "More flambe?" He brandished the dessert deftly onto the table's center. My dreams of friendship flickered, then died, like the flames on the caramelized peaches.

I peeked at Dale, hoping I had not embarrassed him. Dale and I had eloped, despite significant disapproval. Was this bold life choice going to pan out? We came from very different backgrounds...the tectonic plates were already shifting beneath us...would we withstand the "slings and arrows" coming at us from many sides?

Dale met my gaze, smiled, gave me a wink. All was well. Indeed, all would be well. We had taken our vows, "for better, or for worse." Our hearts were one from the very start of this, our Grand Life Adventure. Like a roller-coaster, our Adventure has had its ups and downs.

Yet thirty-six years later, we are still married and blessed with "unconditional" love.

ADELENE ELLENBERG is the author of *Eminent Crimes: A Legal*  *Thriller.* A sequel is underway. She credits CrimeBake, a New England writers' conference, with helping her to hone her writing skills. As an attorney, she draws upon prior legal experiences to develop her plots and characters.

BEAUTY

I'm sitting here with mama.
I'm sitting here in a chair, next to her.
She drinks the decaf, eats the cookie, double chocolate.
I pick at one too.
    Someone wheels over to chat.
    "I love your mom's haircut," she says.
Mom is coaxed and remembers
the elevator ride with the attendant by her side.
Downstairs she must go, to have her hair done, you know.

    She sleeps and wakes in the chair.
Memories not clear.
    Looking at a Santa Claus cut-out,
she declares, "I don't know why
I keep thinking of a fat man."
    A smile hides my surprise.
    "He is fat." I say.
And take her hand.
"I don't know why," she repeats.
"That's okay," I say.

GHOST BELLS AND OTHER HUMANS

The phone rang and I answered it. "I'm sorry," he said. "I broke your flag. This is Fed-Ex. I delivered two packages to your front door. The boxes knocked against the flag and it broke."

"We don't use the front door," I replied, thinking this guy was new. The regular Fed-Ex guy, who was a cutie, knew to bang on the side door.

"I rang your bell; no one answered," new Fed-Ex guy continued.

"The bell doesn't ring," I said. I thought about the reason we disconnected the bell. When we first moved into the house, twenty-six odd years ago, we were greeted with many oddities, including a kid asking me if we were really Indians, of the cowboys and…variety. "Why would you think that?" I had inquired, amused.

"Because your name is Silverfeather."

I can understand how Goldfeder became Silverfeather.

And the bell – it would ring when it was supposed to and continue on and off throughout the day. My husband, Eddie, tried to fix it. And he can fix things. But we gave up, declaring it a "ghost bell." And it remains disconnected to this day.

During this unexpected dialogue, a vastly more significant message was weaving its way to my consciousness and center stage. He made the phone call to say he was sorry. He had a need to heal a wound before it formed. I didn't know he left the packages. And I certainly would not have connected a human hand involved in the breakage. My little flag was faded and way past its prime. It had been handed to me outside Shaw's Supermarket in response to "9-11." I quickly tied it to a bar under the outside light at the end of the driveway with red, white, and blue yarn I'd hastily grabbed out of my closet, because I had to do something. Time, age, and heavy rain would get the blame.

Thank you, fellow human. You made a phone call. It satisfied a need in you. It touched my heart. And I am here to tell you, 'mission accomplished.'

LOVING EMBRACE

Beautiful girl, my Anya is.
Like all grandchildren, she is a wiz.
She greets me with outstretched arms
and a big smile on her face.
I scoop her into my loving embrace.
We play for a while.
She's the mama. I'm the child.
Then we switch.
She's the little sister. I'm the big one.
I'd buy a house near her if I was rich.
Time to search for the cat who ran away to hide,
when three strangers came inside.
"Meow," said the cat.
"What have you done?
"This is my house. I want to have fun."
"Anya, give kitty some tuna," I said.
"Maybe she'll eat and not run."
'Good Girl' – as kitty is called, ran up the stairs
where she was stopped by a gate.
Sitting down on a step accepted her fate.
Daughter and grand-daughter stroked kitty through the bars.
I watched with a smile knowing they'll leave in a day,
going four hundred and thirty-eight miles away.
But my heart has been filled with a joy that will last.
And we'll visit each other again as we've done in the past.

THE PURCHASE: A TRUE STORY

Lillian knew she had to go. There wasn't a second that she thought otherwise. Her decision was made the moment she saw it. And she had to look proper so others wouldn't doubt her ability. The moment to leave her grandparents house had to be timed. No one must know she left. She could not be missed. These were her thoughts as she executed her plan.

Lilly, as people called her, put on a pretty dress. She wore very shiny black leather shoes. A sweater that matched her dress was folded over her arm, and she held a small matching handbag.

The house was quiet when Lilly carefully locked the door of the brick, two-family house and walked two blocks to the trolley stop. It was important that she appear experienced as she pulled herself up onto the step and dropped the fare into the box. When the driver smiled at her, she smiled back. It was 1948 and men could safely smile at a pretty girl.

It was a beautiful spring day. Oh, what a day! The air was fresh and crisp. A perfectly blue sky and a smiling sun added to our "lady's" sense of well-being. It never entered her blond, curly head that her plan wouldn't work. She would photographically remember this day for the rest of her life and smile.

She looked out the window passing the familiar, enjoying the twenty-minute ride. But, when she stepped off the trolley, a slight apprehension filled her body. The blazing sunshine and long empty streets caused butterflies. She was unaccustomed to being alone this far from her family. You must do it, she told herself, and walked as fast as she could to her destination.

"Can I help you young lady?" said the saleslady from behind the counter.

"I want to see that jewelry box," said Lilly pointing.

Putting her hands on a smaller, less expensive box, the sales lady placed it on the counter in front of Lilly. Lillian was upset. She didn't know what she would do if the lady refused to sell her the one she wanted.

"I don't want this one." And to show how smart she was, again she pointed and said, "I like that big pink leather one with gold trim and the pink velvet inside. It's a Mother's Day gift for my mother."

After the saleslady placed the correct box on the counter, Lilly examined it. She was about to say she'd take it, but remembered that her mother taught her to always take a 'fresh one' of anything, one that was wrapped and never handled. So she asked for a new one. And a new one was produced, gift wrapped and placed in a Macy's bag with handles. The saleslady smiled as she took the money and handed Lilly a receipt.

The sun was still shinning as our heroine casually walked back to the trolley stop. Oh! There's one waiting…must catch it, she thought, running.

No one missed her. Why you ask? Didn't they care about her? More than you can imagine. They thought she was in one of the bedrooms playing, outside the house on the porch, or on the sidewalk in front of her grandparents house.

The special day arrived. On Mother's Day, Lillian's mom got the surprise of her life when she unwrapped her gift. Two weeks later, mother and daughter returned to the store and met Lilly's sales lady who enjoyed filling in the details of the purchase.

"I think," said Mother smiling big, "I'll take my five-year old for lunch."

DESTINY

By me, eight-year-old Phyllis Weinstein on a Mother's Day card to my mother. This is the only poem of mine that I automatically memorized, and this is the second time I've written it down. The first time was in the card in 1951.

They told me it was time to be born.
I must choose a mother
and a home to adorn.
I searched all the world
for an angel to love.
Then God gave me you
from up above.

GOING TO MARS

What would I do if I won the lottery? Some people dream of owning yachts, gold toilet seats, diamonds, and private islands, but I would love to have a farm to give homeless families a place to live and work. "Oh look at you," some would say. "You think you're so great and want the world to know how good you are."

Men and, now, women can fight for our country and come home traumatized and homeless. This is a travesty of humanity. When I was growing up, I believed the half-truths that children are taught. Returning soldiers are 'lucky.' The GI Bill ensures them a place to live, the ability to get educated, and provide for a family. Some benefited. Let's be clear. I love the U.S. of A.! I just think we can do better to give all working people, and people trying to work, a place to live and, gee, maybe have a little fun while on "Planet Earth." I've heard that "poverty is big business." Find another business.

I have faith in you, my fellow man,
to give other humans a helping hand.
Find it in your heart to offer a new start.
Yes, some drink too much, you say.
How can we look the other way?
Nourish life on Earth, not search for
past lives on other galaxies and Mars.
Not everyone enjoys sleeping outside
under a bridge, over a grate, next to a
fire in a barrel under the stars.
I have a wonderful year-old car.
I'd buy two new ones for
children who are far.
A new house would be cool.
Helping less fortunate.
The first rule.

What would you do if you won the lottery? Reserve a seat to Mars?

ONE ACT PLAY

"I like your blouse," she says, as she passes by the bed.
And I wonder what's going on in her head.
She pushes the wheelchair around the floor,
enters a room when she comes to a door.
My mom lies in bed. I sit by her side.
Suddenly she notices the lady glide by.
"Who is she?" Mom asks.
"A lady who lives here," I say.
This one-act play
will be repeated another day.
There's someone new in the nursing home.
He dresses nicely.
He has on blue slacks, a white shirt, and a coat.
I ask, "How are you tonight?"
He answers, "I'm off to find a smoke."
"The leaves are changing colors,"
I tell mom with a smile.
She takes my hand, her face aglow.
My chair is pulled close.
We look out the window.

STRETCHING THE MIND

Trying to encourage my brain cells to make new connections by taking classes can be either frustrating or an adventure to pass onto my children. Every time I find myself in a class that isn't quite what I expected, I try to reevaluate the situation.

"Just let it go over your head, Baby," my dad used to say. If I look over my head, a bird will probably poop on my face.

The brochure said, 'Beginner Aerobics.' It was definitely a conspiracy with the sneaker manufacturer because once the class was in progress a new pair was needed by the second session. That's how fast you moved. I think it was called beginner because the rest of the class, including the instructor, needed a good laugh before the real class. And after the beginners dropped out over the course of a few weeks, there was more room for the serious exercise freaks. By this time, no one could get their money back. And speaking about the instructor, who is this person? Where is the one listed in the brochure? Oh, she couldn't make it, now that we couldn't get our money back. More smiles.

I had chosen Tuesday night to take yoga, instead of Thursday night, because the previous instructor of thirty-plus years retired, and the brochure said that she recommended her replacement. I was a happy camper when an hour of yoga went by and I was thrilled with our new teacher. Then she decided to enlighten us even more by stating that she's the Thursday night instructor. They had switched nights. This is getting to be a habit. But this habit turned out to be good.

Sometimes I take a class and wonder why the 'fairy-godmother of education' has done this to me. And I realize it's to test and retest my ability to overcome the credulous. And to send me off to Barnes and Noble or Borders bookstore for a few days. Capitalism and education definitely do go hand in hand. In the bookstores, I learn what I suspected all along. My instructor wants to get out of the house and is bored to tears with this beginner. I wish that I didn't have to be a beginner. But I have to start someplace. Maybe next time I'll learn first and take the class second.

I don't know where to go from here. If I could, I'd learn everything. Now I don't know if I could or couldn't learn everything. I only know that I'd be a beginner. And some 'beginner classes' don't like that.

ESCAPE OF THE BABBLING BROOK

"You babble like a babbling brook," the husband shouted.

The abused woman drifted into the shelter of her woods. Tip-toeing across the stones, she waded into the brook. Knees perched high like small mountains, she squatted. Her backside almost touching the water.

I watched her as she moved her right hand over the stones. It was difficult to see if her palm touched the water, wetting it. The air around us became light and smelled wonderfully fresh. I had a desire to breathe in until my lungs and body could hold no more. The stillness around us was eerie. Seeing her lift her left hand so that it rested on her right knee, almost perpendicular to the stone bed, made me stand motionless lest I break the spell or stop her. Her movements were barely noticeable until they reached fruition.

The kind man came and knelt on the other side of the brook, mirroring her position. He smiled at her, tilting his head as one does when kissing. And she did the same. Separated by five feet of flowing water and stones, they kissed.

"Most of us are not like him," the kind man said. "You have a choice. You can be the flowing brook, babbling and babbling, enjoying the wonders of its journey. Or you can be a stone, washed upon and embedded."

The others approached her. They were women from all over the globe. Some were dressed in their native clothes. It was their choice. There were men, too. But not from every country.

Her husband ran out of the house towards her, stopping just outside the huge circle of people.

"She's beyond our world now," I said, stepping out of the shadows and looking into his angry eyes. Tears ran down his face.

The crowd moved away from the brook, revealing a drab-colored bird and a brightly-colored one. They were preening, getting ready to take flight.

As they lifted into the air, a small gold ring fell from the drab-colored one and landed in the brook. Her husband knelt down, tears still streaming, put his hand into the cool water and palmed the ring. When he stood and opened his hand, a feather flew out, landed in the brook, and was carried away.

THE THERMOSTAT CONTROLLER EDITOR

Do you believe in the healing power of music? Do you believe in the glory of friendship? Do you believe in phone calls that can stop your heart? Do you believe in the supernatural?

In 2001, I received such a phone call from my brother Martin's wife.

"The paramedics are here working on Marty." Without skipping a beat, she continued, "He just died." He had a heart attack which was masked by the pain of passing kidney stones. He was 59.

I packed for an overnight stay, left my husband and two small daughters at home, hopped on a "shuttle," and headed for Queens, NY. I stayed for a week. He was twelve years older than his wife and not an easy man to live with. In the 1950s, no one knew how to recognize an intelligently gifted child. He was a handful at home and in school. But, when he wasn't threatening or "shadow boxing" me, he delighted me and our parents with his stories. After witnessing his performances as the lead in most school plays, why didn't someone mentor him instead of ignoring his high IQ scores and refuse to let him skip a grade. He put himself through college at age 28. I can still feel the joy of watching my big brother perform on stage in our school auditorium.

‡ ‡ ‡

Not a single question is on my mind as I pull the kitchen door shut and get into my heated car on the chilly evening of March 9, 2011. Driving an easy half hour SE takes me to Bridgewater, MA, where four members of "The Tale Spinners" writing group pile into my car. Motor running, I wait.

"Hi. How ya doin?"

"Is everyone here?"

"Who's sitting up front?"

"Okay. I'll get in the middle."

Winter coats make them very cozy in the backseat, where I'll be in someone else's car next time. Pleasant conversation all around and encouragement for Christine. I'm feeling kind of neutral about the evening but looking forward to dinner. Maybe seafood?

We arrive. Park. Get out. In a few months, the huge parking lot across the street will fill up with tourists and locals. Tonight, the dim streetlights cast shadows accentuating the cold gloom and stark barrenness. Even now, I can "see" and "feel" the atmosphere outside the Waterfront Bar and Grill at The Village Landing. We walk inside.

POW!! There's enough light and energy to excite Tesla. Square tables are packed together. Most are filled with writers, either accomplished or hopeful. Christine's husband Mike, his brother Joe, and Christine sit at the table next to me.

Someone says, "I'm chilly."

There's a chorus of, "Me too."

"I should've brought a sweater."

There's a thermostat on the wall behind Mike. Christine glances at it. Hmmm? Does it work?

It's 'Open Mic' night, and now it's time for Christine to entertain us. She delights the room by wearing a visor type head piece that when she flips the front flap up reads, "Editor." Her story is received well, and she embraces the applause as she returns to her table.

The band begins to fill the room with music. Four acoustic guitars play. We listen. The packed crowd listens, tapping feet and listening. The musicians keep the rhythm and we sway to the familiar song.

Christine examines the thermostat.

Behind me, wind coming off the bay blows through the window. The song changes, picking up the pace. And we bounce to the beat, moving up and down, back and forth like a dance.

She raises the numbers on the thermostat.

Adelene, opposite me, slaps her hands on her lap, up, down, up, down to the electrifying beat. Beside me, the Thermostat Controller's brother-in-law beats his foot against the floor. Hands, feet, bodies move to the music.

The thermostat is turned down. She turns away from the wall and smiles. Her eyes shine, and her smile lights up her face. She's the editor of her fate and the reason they piled into my car. Her 'Open Mic' performance drew us to her and The Waterfront.

He sings, "I wish I was....," and I don't care that I no longer can understand the words. The music is like the joy of fishing on Chesapeake Bay.

Joe informs me that the thermostat was on air conditioning mode.

"Okay," I say.

And the singer sings, nicely.

Music's too loud again. I shove the tissues back into my ears.

Adelene tells me, "That's the snare drum" that's snaring my ear drums. Boom, boom, it marks time.

I turn from her sweet smile to look at the empty Plymouth street. Darkness is the inlet's friend and street lights illuminate the restaurants and a hug parking lot. A sign reported that we can park for free until the season begins.

"The windows are new," states Nancy.

"You're right," I answer, placing my hand against the window pane. "No draft. Just cold," I say.

I continue looking out of the window. Through the reflection of my hand, I see a figure. A few seconds pass before I recognize him. He smiles and throws me a kiss. No longer hearing the music, peace and contentment fill my body. I smile at him knowing he can see into my loving heart. Marty is standing on the other side of the glass looking like anyone who would stand outside. After about thirty seconds, still smiling, he slowly backs away from the window and drifts into the darkness.

Turning from the window, I smile back at Nancy. We sit quietly as the music winds down. The musicians begin to pack their instruments. Others put on outerwear or make a quick trip to the bathroom. This was my first experience going with the group to this type of event. Kind words are aimed at me: "Good to meet you." "I hope to see you again." "Did you have a good time?" I answer, "Same here," "Me too," "Yes."

My little group is also content. I can tell by the chatter that begins again in the car as I reverse direction. Good nights and see you soon, door openings and closings complete this "leg of the trip."

In my heart, I was not alone as I drove home. It was filled with the glory of friendship and good will. I looked forward to next time. And there were many next times. Lucky me.

Postscript: Please read, The Thermostat Controller Editor's story about her special night, under the author C. Quigley Muratore.

PHYLLIS GOLDFEDER can teach. Her BA and Master classes  made that officially possible. She's managed her own business and given financial seminars. May began twelve years as a museum educator. Time is spent experimenting by creating art, organic gardening, cooking, and learning about scientific theories. Joys are family, friends, and kitty.

THE ACCIDENTAL WEAVER

I became a weaver by accident...literally.

One ordinary afternoon in 1987, I went to mail a letter. As I sat waiting for a parking space in front of the post-office, a truck rear-ended my car. Several weeks later, I had emergency open heart surgery – still wearing my neck and back brace.

This was just days before my fortieth birthday.

Physical therapy became my occupation.

I took up hand quilting for diversion from pain. My project, a quilt for our queen-sized bed, required a large whole cloth for backing. Unable to find just the right shade of blue, I was eventually referred to the Braid Aide Fabric store in Pembroke.

At the check-out, I noticed a small room to one side. The room was empty except for a row of wooden forms lined up like railroad cars against the wall. Three walls of the perimeter were shelves that held cones of wool and balls of colorful cotton.

"What goes on back there?" I asked the clerk.

"Oh, that's where the weaving lessons take place," she told me.

When I was a girl, I remember my mother and grandmother would tear old cotton bed sheets into one-and-a-half-inch strips. They would wind them into large balls to be delivered to "The Weaver." I never met "The Weaver," nor saw her loom, but the huge box of balls was always returned to us transformed into beautiful, thick, white, fringed, throw rugs.

As I gazed into that neat weaving room, a memory washed over me of the hours of fun my cousins and I had "riding" the rugs like sleds down the staircase from the third floor to the second of Grandma's house. The sled was made by sitting on half of the rug and pulling the other half taut, enabling the sled to fly, barely touching each step. It was with this memory that something in me stepped up and declared, "I want to weave."

Not even knowing what weaving lessons entailed, I was drawn to the strange looking contraptions and placed my name on a short waiting list.

My bed quilt was immediately turned into a twelve-inch pillow top; and my quilt needle and thimble were abandoned for shuttles and weaving bobbins.

I've always loved school. I arrived on my first day of weaving class like an eager nine-year-old. I carried my basket with scissors, tape measure, notebook, pencil, and fishing weights. Everyone always asks why fishing weights, but you'll have to attend Class #6, "How to Repair A Broken Warp Thread," to understand.

I was told to arrive at 6:30 PM. The other students were already there, having arrived at 6 PM to set up. They had their looms pulled away from the wall and were busy doing various activities such as warping, threading, weaving, winding bobbins, and gossiping. I was already familiar with the gossiping part.

My teacher, Jeanne, a tall soft-spoken blonde with a mid-western accent, was perched on the corner of a metal desk talking about her new-born, diapers, and night feedings. She introduced me to the other five students.

Then she said to me, "I like my new students to weave a sampler first." She directed me to a shelf with possibly 100 spools of "Maysville" carpet warp. Each spool contained 800 yards of 100% cotton. I learned to love Maysville. It's strong, smooth, and comes in lots of gorgeous colors, shades, and hues.

"Choose two colors," I was instructed. "For contrast, pick a light and a dark."

I didn't know how important a decision this was supposed to be, and I spent far too much time picking a dark blue and a pale yellow.

"Okay, since we are running a little behind, let's just skip the math part and get over to the warping board. Usually," Jeanne continued, "I would go over how to figure the amount of thread needed to build your warp and weft, but we'll do that another day."

Considering the amount of muscle relaxant I was still on, that was a good decision. Also, my mind was much clearer at 8 AM than at 8 PM. Jeanne recited the formula to figure the number of threads required, and I nodded, glassy-eyed, and didn't bother to memorize it.

So I made my first warp. You actually have to figure out each thread in the fabric. Who knew? I didn't. The warp is the threads on the loom. The actual weaving part of weaving is easy. Preparing the warp and weft and dressing the loom are not.

I spent the rest of this lesson and the following weeks making my first warp. As I stood before the warping board, swaying back and forth from dowel to dowel, I reassured myself that I could accomplish this even though I had serious doubts.

Many of the weaving tasks I found difficult to master, and physically many of the motions were painful for me. I was discouraged a lot, but I persevered, reminding myself about the jackknife.

When I was a teenager, I wanted to do the jackknife off the diving board. For most of the summer, two or three times a week, I dove and dove, over and over; always belly flopping. My thighs and stomach were bruised black and blue. Then one night, I dreamed that I succeeded. The following day I did it for real: a perfect jackknife.

Anything new, practice until you can do it in your sleep – it works!

Weaving didn't come easily to me. Nor was it cheap. My husband still refers to my sampler as the $295 oversized pot holder. I made every mistake that could possibly be made. I'm certain that if there were a contest, I would win "messiest" ever produced.

It's been decades since that first weaving lesson. Sometimes when a beginner weaver is discouraged, I pull out my sample. It always seems to help.

Now weaving is part of my identity. I've heard people say, "Christine is my weaver friend."

Today, I'm working toward having them say, "Christine is my writer friend who also weaves."

FACE IN THE WINDOW
(excerpt from novel in progress)

My story begins on my grandparent's farm in Southern Ohio. North Heck Hill borders the farm at its base. The Southern Plantation-style home, constructed from bricks formed and baked on the property, was built in the late 1800s.

On this particular warm summer day, my cousins and I, all of us between the ages of eleven and fourteen, decided to organize a sleepover at Grandma's. We arrived early, claimed bedrooms, and put our "luggage" away. Luggage is grandiose for what we actually brought: a toothbrush, comb, and pajamas. Since none of us lived more than a mile or so from Grandma's farm, little else was needed, except maybe a sweater, a change of underwear or a pair of shorts, shoes or jeans, just in case.

We spent the entire day doing what I call "leaning on the cow fence." We reminisced, like old folks, about all the good times we had. We sat on the fence by the horse trough and laughed about the time we "swam" in the trough then hung our clothes on bushes to dry.

We remembered spending days doing forbidden play in the barn. One hot summer day we threw a rope over a second-floor beam. We climbed onto a stack of hay bales that we had placed just so. Then, taking turns, we grabbed the end of the dangling rope and jumped from the hayloft, swung through the air across the width of the barn, out the upper level doors over the cow yard. We would whoop and yell for each other. The only skill needed was to judge when to let go and fall into the thoughtfully placed pile of loose straw in the cows' yard. That day ended when Linda successfully dropped the two stories, only slightly misjudged the distance to the pile of straw at the bottom, and landed knee deep in mud and cow poop.

We all knew it would be trouble if our parents figured out what we did all day those long-ago summers. We also knew that our parents had also played in the barn exactly the same way. One of my favorite games was building houses and tunnels in the hay loft. We never had a cave-in. Although we knew the danger, we built anyway; and we were good engineers, stacking and placing huge bales of hay to build a clubhouse. I don't remember ever having a "meeting" in the clubhouse. It was just one of many projects that filled the carefree days.

We laughed about the time when we teased the "old bull." He treed us in the upper pasture and kept us there until supper time.

We spent most of the day watching the small herd of brown, white-faced Hereford cows. We watched the cows chew their cud. We watched them, and they watched us with their big black eyes.

It's amazing how fate arranges events. All the cousins were there that night: Linda and her sister Sally; Judy and her brothers, Bob, Don, and Joe; my sister Kathy and me; and Jane with her sister Mary.

We all took up residence on the third floor. The boys went off to get some sleep; they were planning to work in the early morning mowing around flower beds and the lane ditches. Linda, Judy, Jane, and I started telling ghost stories designed to clear the room of the younger girls.

Soon Sally, Kathy, and Mary went to another bedroom. Jane, as usual, fell asleep quickly. That left Linda, Judy, and me. Around midnight, Linda said she was hungry, so she and I decided to raid the refrigerator. Judy remained behind in case Jane woke up.

Linda took the flashlight and we descended the three steps to the top landing, then the thirteen stairs down to the second floor. We tiptoed down the hall past our snoring grandparents' bedroom. Here, at the end of the immense hall, at the back of the house, were three doors: Grandma's bedroom door, a door to the backyard – since the house is built into the hill it opened to the outside, and a third door leading to the stairwell that went downstairs to the main level. There, a white porcelain potty sat on a small braided throw rug along with a half roll of toilet paper. As long as any of us could remember, this little convenience corner appeared whenever a child was an overnight guest. With no indoor plumbing yet, the outhouse was still in use year round.

The potty was always gone by morning.

The stairwell, unlike modern staircases, had a lockable door at the top, a large landing, very deep, very wide stairs, and solid plaster walls. The only opening was at the bottom in the living room. The opening was so wide that if you wanted to block it for some reason, a full-sized hutch cabinet would be needed.

As quietly as possible, Linda and I entered the stairwell to the main floor. After we shut the door, we turned on the light and quickly descended with Linda in the lead.

Four steps from the bottom, Linda came to an abrupt halt. I nearly knocked her over.

"What's that?" she whispered, pointing to the living room windows now visible at the front of the house.

"Looks like Sally," I said.

"That's not Sally!"

"I don't mean your sister; I mean Sally, our cow. It looks like her with that white face and those big black eyes." To me the image looked like our favorite cow, Sally, even though I knew that the cows were safely in the barn for the night.

"Why would the cows come to the house and look in?" Linda asked. "It's not Sally. It's not a cow."

My mind was searching for answers. "We watched them all day, now it's their turn to watch us."

"Maybe it's a reflection," Linda whispered.

"Yes, maybe that's it. If we shut off the light in the stairwell, we'll see that it's just an illusion."

If we could bring ourselves to descend three more steps, we could reach the switch at the bottom. Clinging to each other, we slowly moved to the left-hand wall.

Why, at this point, we didn't run upstairs to wake our grandparents, I don't know. They were sleeping in the bedroom across from the stairwell. Surely, they would have protected us and run off any intruders. It simply didn't occur to either of us.

We slowly inched down the last three stairs, hand-in-hand, keeping our eyes on the image in the window. We were shivering slightly even though it was a warm summer night.

Linda slowly extended her arm and reached for the switch. She pushed the toggle down and we were plunged into total darkness.

Linda had put out the light hoping that the face would disappear. But when our eyes adjusted, the face was even CLEARER.

"This is not good. Turn it back on. Turn it back on!" I had lost some cool.

"What do we do now?" Linda's voice was developing an edge.

"I don't know; just don't look in its eyes," I said. Where I got that idea, I don't know.

"What? Why? That's not Sally you know!"

Things were starting to get bizarre and about to escalate. Linda's mantra became, "That's not Sally, you know. That's not a cow."

My counter-mantra was, "Don't look at its eyes."

I think, however, we had already been looking at its eyes too long.

"What should we do?" we asked together.

"I don't know," Linda answered.

"I think we should just walk through the house as if it were not there," I said.

"What?" Linda rocked from foot to foot.

"Don't worry," I said, "they won't come in unless we say it's okay." Where I got that idea from, I don't know. Perhaps from a movie, or maybe from the eyes of the face itself.

"How do you know that? That's not a cow," Linda said again.

"I don't know why I think they won't come in, but I'm pretty sure they won't. Is the front door locked?"

We crossed through the living room on the way to the kitchen. I kept saying, "Pretend you don't see it. Watch it out of the corner of your eye. Don't look at it."

The main floor of the house is one giant room. A previous owner had decided two rooms were better than one and installed a waist-high wall with a foot-wide shelf at countertop height. This made for a full view of both the living room and the kitchen no matter where you stood.

"What do you see, exactly?" Linda asked.

"I see something, Lindy. What do you see?"

Slowly, she said, "I see a white….face …..eyes….."

"Lindy, don't look at the eyes. Maybe we're just having hallucinations," I offered.

"Can we both have the same hallucination?" she asked.

"I don't know, but I'm sure I've heard of it before. Lindy, I need you to do something. I'm going to see if the door is locked. I want you to stand here and watch out of the corner of your eye. If it moves, or does anything, let me know fast."

This was important because only a couple of feet separated the door from the window, the window with the face.

Then for reasons I can't explain, I dropped to my hands and knees and crawled to the front door.

"Can you still see it, Linda?"

"Yes."

"I'm going to reach up and turn on the porch light. Maybe the light will scare it away…Lindy, I'm afraid."

"Me too," she said. "Go ahead, I'll keep looking. It's not a cow, you know."

I'm sure Linda is in trouble. She has said "It's not a cow" far too many times.

I couldn't reach the switch from the floor, so I popped up, flipped the switch, then squatted back down in front of the solid bottom half.

"Lindy?"

A slight moan.

"Lindy, what happened?"

"It's worse."

"What happened? Did it move? You were supposed to tell me if it moved."

"There are more."

"On the porch? Oh, my God!"

"Yes, and down by the cars, too!"

"Down by the cars? How can you see down there? Aren't you shielding your eyes?"

"When you turned on the light, it lit up the driveway, too. There are three more down there."

"What are they doing?"

"They're just standing there under the driveway light."

"What should I do? Should I shut the light off?"

"I don't know. Is the door locked?"

I was kneeling behind the solid half of the front door with the lock right at my face.

"Is it locked?" Linda urged again.

I was faced with an ordinary, everyday object that I had never paid any particular attention to until that moment.

Was it locked? I couldn't tell. The lock, 1800's style, a black cast iron box the size of a very thin paperback book on its side, had a keyhole but no key. I realized the locking device was a lever on the top of the box The lever was to the right.

"Left or right, Lindy, how do I tell which is locked?"

"Try it."

"Okay, but this time watch and let me know if anything moves! And, remember, don't look at its eyes."

To test, I reached over, turned the large porcelain doorknob and pulled. The door moved toward me. The click of the latch and the rattle of the screen door, then the click of the latch again, as I quickly pushed the door shut seemed abnormally loud.

Wrong! That must be to open.

With shaking fingers, I reached and pushed the lever to the left. Click. Then I turned the cold white knob and pulled the door again. Click. Rattle. Click. Wrong again! My whole body was shaking. I moved the lever to the right one more time, and pulled. Click. Rattle.

Click!

"Oh, no! It's broken; it won't lock!"

Then, loud enough for whoever or whatever was standing outside to hear, I said, "Okay! All locked!"

I crawled a few feet away from the door, stood, and nonchalantly, walked toward Linda who was still standing between the two rooms. At least I hoped it was nonchalant. By now I was no longer sure that they would not enter uninvited. I took a furtive glance to see the three figures shimmering in the driveway light.

"Okay, Lindy," I loudly declared, "let's look in the fridge and get back upstairs."

We hesitated: the refrigerator was all the way across the kitchen. You couldn't get any further away from the safety of the stairwell. There the fridge stood, in the center of the left wall. A 1950 model Philco. About five feet tall, white, rounded corners, all curves, no sharp edges.

Pretending that nothing was amiss, we walked across the kitchen and opened the refrigerator door. The door opened from left to right and we stuck our heads inside where we could talk "privately"; the door shielding the view of the back windows.

"They're at the back windows too, Chrissie. Did you see? Did you see?"

"Yes, one in each window."

"We'd better get back upstairs."

"Okay, but let's make sure the back door is locked first."

Even though Linda wanted to head straight upstairs, she reluctantly agreed to be my lookout while I checked the kitchen door.

"Linda, you pretend to get a drink of water from the bucket while I check the lock."

A white bucket with drinking water was always kept on a wooden utility table by the door to the summer house. We all drank from a tin cup that hung from the rim of the water bucket.

We closed the refrigerator and attempted a casual walk to the bucket at the backdoor. A knot began to form in my belly. I realized that the kitchen door had no lock.

We would have to go out into the summer house to latch the outside back door.

Attached to the main house is a large addition, although it was probably built at the same time. My German grandma called it "SummerHaus."

My knees were weak and sweat was trickling down my body under my cotton nightgown. I remember thinking, "This must be how an animal feels sensing that there is a predator just outside." But at least I could lock my door.

There was no way Linda was going to come with me into the summer house. She would stand "lookout." She would wait in the kitchen. It was dark in the summer house, but we agreed that we had to be sure that the door was latched and locked.

"Should we turn the light on?"

"No!" Not a good idea. I could find my way.

"I'll just check the latch and run right back." I assured Linda I wouldn't need a light, it's only eight or nine steps to the door. A door we used all day, every day, to get to the backyard, to the henhouse and the outhouse.

I opened the solid door to the summer kitchen and stepped down two steps.

I stopped for a moment to compose myself with a deep breath in and out. I turned left and took two baby steps. The cistern pump handle was on my left. Three, four, five steps more, and I reached out and touched the lid of Grandma's old wringer washer to my right. A sixth, then a seventh giant step, the utility table. Now eight and I'm at the door to the backyard.

As I fumbled to secure the hook and eye latch, a dread crept over me. I remembered that there were two other outside doors in the summer house. The first was directly across from the kitchen door. It led to the woodhouse. The other was to the right of the kitchen door. It led to the front yard. We rarely used either of those doors.

I placed the hook over the eye...a light touch on my shoulder...I was not alone.

HOW TO SURVIVE THE SCARIEST THREE MINUTES OF YOUR LIFE
(while heckled by your inner editor)

Your interest is piqued when your writing group rehashes their most recent poetry readings. You're invited to the next event, coincidentally a mere two weeks away.

You don't need poetry. Prose will do. Just limit yourself to three minutes. You can do that.

Scour your stash of short stories for an appropriate piece.

Select a chapter from your "Alien Abduction" memoir.

Practice for hours reading to the microwave timer, all the while cutting sentence after sentence from your manuscript to get it down to the three-minute limit.

Perform for your husband. He slows you down. You cut more sentences. He counsels, "People will talk and order drinks. They'll walk around. Just don't stop."

‡ ‡ ‡

On the day of the event, you, your husband, his brother and wife dine on fresh fried fish at a wharf restaurant nearby.

Arrive early at the bar. Get good seats. Your husband and his brother will look around. They'll elbow poke each other, asking, "Where's Dobie Gillis and Maynard G. Crebbs?"

Tell your sister-in-law you really aren't that nervous – might be better if you were.

Sign the Cable TV release form. Agree to go on first. Your inner editor shows up at this very moment to announce, in a very ominous voice;"Ahh Oooh…The front car of a scary roller coaster ride!"

Listen to the band. Everyone's in a festive mood. Don't drink. You don't want alcohol to blame for any flop.

The MC introduces you. You walk confidently to the stage, an imaginary area the size of your kitchen table. It's cluttered with drums, huge speakers, instruments on stands, all strung together with cords on the floor and draped to and fro in the air. You're relieved you don't have claustrophobia.

No turning back now! The roller coaster safety bar is locked!

My God, you think, what am I doing! But you hear yourself reading in a clear, though quivering voice. You begin to shake. Your papers move so much you can't read.

The coaster car chugs up the high hill, shaking and straining for the top.

Don't stop. You hold your notes with two hands. You pray the paper doesn't rip under the pressure. Don't stop. Suddenly you notice a podium to your left. You reach out to steady yourself. Just as suddenly, you realize it's too far…

"Keep your hands in the moving car at all times," the editor commands!

Don't stop. You can still hear your voice. You are on time.

The car grinds, and moans, and shakes all the way; finally reaches the top of the hill. It pauses a long moment, teetering, teetering…

You dare to peek at the audience. No one is drinking, talking, or walking around. They are on the edge of their seats listening intently.

What do you expect? They think you are about to faint!

It's all downhill from here.

The wind is in your face. Your hair blows happily behind you. The car pulls up to the platform. *The attendant helps you out of the car.*

The MC takes your arm. You enjoy the applause.

It's over – the scariest three minutes of your life!

"Let's do it again!" you and your editor shout silently in unison. *"Let's do it again!"*

CHRISTINE QUIGLEY MURATORE compares her thirty years as a fiber artist to her recent incarnation as a writer. "No need to change vocabulary," she says. "I'm still fabricating yarns and organizing threads of words or cloth whether at the loom, spinning wheel, or computer keyboard.

A LOVE AFFAIR

Beach days by Nancy Byron *are here again; the salt, the sun, the sand*
Putting on my flip flops, it really feels so grand!
Gazing at the ocean, breathing in the air
Sea gulls and crabs around me, what a love affair!
Wiggling my toes in the sand, splashing in the sea
Reading a romance novel, whatever pleases me.
Searching for shells and other things, fills me with delight
Finding hidden sea treasures, that are buried beyond my sight.
Endless hours of looking, for the sparkle of colored glass
To put in my bucket and bring home at last.
Lounging in my chair, I watch the kids at play
The sun is hot upon me; could there be a better day?
Ice cream and french fries sound like a plan
Then back to my chair, to work on my tan.
Bikini-clad girls, in suits far too tight
Muscular boys, try to show off their might.
Boats are riding on the waves, the wind is softly blowing
I'm at a place of peace and rest, I have an inner knowing
The rhythm of life, plays out at the shore
I sense the eternal,
    nothing less,
    nothing more.
A love affair I'm
    having; for me,
    there is no end
Countless days at the
    beach
There, my time, I'll
    spend!

BACK IN THE DAY

Things were different, back in the day
Kids , seen and not heard, go off to play.
"Be home by supper" , Mom would say.
Neighbors helped each other and really cared
No one was all alone and scared.
Doors left unlocked, doctors came to the home
Grandpa lived with us, kids got to roam.
A feeling of trust and good intent
People loved one another, wherever they went.
It's a different day now, more evil and greed
Watch out for the children, folks don't get what they need.
"Love one another," a wise man said
Share with each other, your water and bread.
Make the world better by your being here
When you meet the Lord, there's nothing to fear!

MAGESTIC

Do trees listen when when I cry
And bend toward me
To wonder why
They are majestic and strong
Perhaps they hear my mournful song
As a kid, I climbed up high
Perched on a branch in the sky
Breathing in all the smells
Never fearing if I fell
Standing tall after the rain
Do they feel happy, do they feel pain
Protecting birds and their nests
Speaking of wisdom and timelessness
Soft as an easy chair
In winter, their limbs lay bare
Naked for all to see
Surely I think the trees hear me

THE GOLD BOX

I have a gold box and in it are cards,
Of sorrow and sympathy
Just like glass shards.
They cut me, they pierce me
They beckon me too
To relive all of the moments I had with you.
"It's a joke," you say and I'm laughing hard
You've taken me away from that piercing shard.
I put it away, it's too much to bear
It will be there forever, with sorrow and despair.
One day I'll pick it up, when I sense it's time
And scream and cry and remember
When that little boy was mine!

AT WHAT PRICE BOUGHT

At what price bought is my growing soul
Is grief always a big black hole?
Within grief can be seeds of hope, seeds of change and inner growth
Crying, yes, and sadness too
Maybe grief can bring something new
A softness, a stirring, a vague new thought
A space, an opening
But at what price bought?
Love never dies, nor the remembrance of you
I am on a journey to find something new

GREG'S JOURNEY

Like soldiers on guard, your friends stood around you
To surround you with love and strength and tears.
What a moment it was, to remember those years
And know that life will continue on.
As the sweet smell of lilacs in the air,
Their briefness of life, is so like your own.
Here for a while and suddenly gone,
I still see your smile, your spirit is with me.
Those cheek kisses give me such warmth,
Like the rays of the sun peeking through.
So handsome you lay, wearing a shirt of blue
Like the sky at a lingering dawn.
The hands that worked so hard in life
Remained silent and unmoving.
A last kiss and hug
Till we meet again, my son.

GREG'S LETTER

I'm not there in the ground like a plant or a tree
I'm around you, Mum,
Can't you see?
I'm in the wind and the sky
That part of me can never die
Can you hear me laughing and feel me near?
I'm hugging you now
No need for your tears
My things that you can't bear to give up
I don't need them now
It's all just stuff
I know it all reminds you of me
But I'm with you, Mum,
Can't you see?
My spirit is as close as your breath
Don't worry, Mum,
There is no death
I'm not lost
I'm in God's care
Don't cry at my grave
I'm not there

Nancy Byron

MY HEART WILL STILL SING

I'm not giving up on God
just yet;
I want answers, answers to your death.
A whole life ahead,
I cannot see
Why God took you away from me.
It seems so final, an awful thing
And yet I think my heart will still sing.
When I remember you, I laugh and smile;
Knowing God gave you to me for a while.
The shadow of death will never win,
God still triumphs over death and sin.

THE SWELL

I truly thought I was doing well
Then it knocked me over – the greatest swell
of grief and anguish
it caught me off guard
Like an undertow, pulling me hard.
Trying to fight it, I know I won't win
It's too powerful, too mighty, sucking me in.
To let go is madness, to give up is a 'NO'
Yet, I decide, I have to let go.
It takes me out and pulls me down, let go, let go
Now all is calm.
I'm able to breathe, I'm afloat somewhere
But where am I going with you not there?
There is a force much greater than me, that carries me along
Until the shore I see.
Battered and bruised but still alive, I'm pushed along
By the fearsome tide.
There, I've survived, I'm doing well
Until comes along another swell.

NANCY BYRON nurtures her creative spirit by writing poetry,  painting, and drawing. She graduated from Nazareth College of Rochester. Her children and grandchildren are constant sources of inspiration as well as the ocean and all of nature. She resides on the South Shore of MA with her husband, Jim.

Preface

The following material are excerpts taken from a book I am putting together about the remarkable life-affirming experience of a small family with a profoundly handicapped child. Titled *Love's Race in Three Voices*, it is written through the voices of Greg's father Barry, his older brother Matthew, and the words of his late mother Sharon. Whenever the author changes, his or her name is noted in parentheses. I hope that the reader will also find these words to be a life-affirming expression.

UNCONDITIONAL LOVE

(Barry)

The glow of fall's color in a small New England town, the thunderous crashing of an ocean wave across a sandy beach before a storm, the unbridled joy of a little dog seeing her best friend step off the home-coming school bus; moments etched somewhere deep within us, and somehow beyond the ordinary limits of time.

As brilliant and soul-touching as these moments are, they pale in contrast to the experience of taking care of our profoundly handicapped son, Gregory David. During his twenty-two years with us, our little family of four glowed through the power of one powerless in every way, except the ability to draw and give love. This was the gift which grounded the rest of us: a dedicated, intelligent, and strongly intuitive mother, Sharon; an older brother, Matthew, a warrior of the heart; and myself, the father who often considered himself the luckiest person in the world.

It may seem strange for one who has lost a beloved son to make such a suggestion; that is, to consider himself most fortunate. But, if you have ever observed how people can be so totally free in front of a little baby, trying to get the infant to interact and smile, then you will begin to understand my suggestion. There is no rejection, no judgment or conditional acceptance from the infant; just pure unabashed love. For over twenty-two years, through easy times, through scores of hospitalizations, and through the full range of otherwise 'normal' endeavors, our family bloomed. Somewhere, deep within each of us, time itself stopped and paid reverence, basking in the magnificent display of love, totally free.

I cannot begin to convey a picture of 'totally free' in any objective sense. It would not do justice to the reality of our experience. This would be more fittingly the stuff of poets and other lovers of truth. I can do no better than to present a portrait penned by his brother at the age of fourteen. Sitting at Greg's bedside during one of his hospitalizations, Matt and his mother together allowed love to be the artist:

The Giver

(Matthew & Sharon)

"My brother, Gregory, is like a shadow that touches the edges of people's lives. He moves by gently, almost imperceptibly. His presence never intrudes, never clings, never seeks dominion. As he freely passes through boundaries without setting off alarms, his spirit energizes those spaces he leaves behind. Most remarkably, Gregory implants an invisible seed in fertile souls, an empowering seed that can only be deposited by those as powerless as he. Its issue is as unobtrusive as the one who leaves this gift. This seed is love, undemanding love. It germinates and grows nourished by the fond yet unformed memory of once being touched by the softness of its giver.

My brother, the giver, is paralyzed and retarded. Cerebral palsy is the faceless enemy that claimed him victim. Maybe in this time of "let's help him develop to his fullest potential" that doesn't sound so comprehensive. But I'm not talking about the poster child who looks up with sparkling "Help-me-become-all-that-I-can-be" eyes. Gregory is completely helpless, as helpless as any human being can be. Gregory cannot walk, cannot sit, cannot talk, cannot see, and cannot eat. His world is a place of formless images, disconnected sounds, feeding tubes, medicines, and water mattresses. He has seizures that make him lapse, breathless, into a limbo of unconsciousness. And yet Gregory lives.

Gregory's over-sized head is covered with thick, darkly silken hair that glistens in the sunlight. His large, liquid, brown eyes contrast starkly against almost translucent skin that remains free of blemish or marking. He is thirteen but looks five. He never grows. Gregory's thin little arms end in diminutive, transparent ET fingers that allow the light to pass through them. He often reaches up to touch something heavenward that only he can see. Description alone of his features

88

conjures up tragic images of Tiny Tim caught in a time warp. But what I see of the Gregory who lies before me stops far short of who he has revealed himself to be.

Gregory is the only human I know who, although he can do nothing else, allows me to completely be the person I am. No expectations, no demands, no disappointment, no wanting more. When I touch his shoulder, or kiss his cheek, or speak his name, Gregory turns in my direction and smiles deeply, knowingly. All concept of time is suspended when we are together. He has nothing yet everything to give me in this acknowledgment that he just enjoys being with me. Gregory's calm, his gentleness and purity of spirit, seeps into my heart. Serenity replaces weariness.

Gregory's great gift to me is the knowledge that I am able to love him just the way he is. I no longer think of what might have been or grieve for what is lost. I no longer feel that Gregory is someone who needs to be fixed. Gregory is "who he is," in the present tense, the now. What is gained – this quiet, gentle moment, this laughter, this celebration of being – is more than many ever know. In this instant, life bursts forth from the kernel of joy Gregory implants in a hidden chamber of my heart. He then allows me to leave him and bring that energy and love into the world that he will never see or know. I return transformed, renewed. The love I share with Gregory expands my heart beyond the universe. I know that I am becoming more than I might have been if I had never known him.

What Gregory gives me, I give away. Strangely, the well never empties. It is continually replenished. And I find that each time I return to Gregory, he teaches me again that, while I will always be in the process of becoming, he has arrived. Gregory is already all that he can be. I lose nothing that passes through me to others. Love renews itself as long as I am continually willing to accept it, and then allow it flow out from me.

There are those who cannot bear to look upon my brother's face. They see only brokenness and suffering and cannot bear the pain it causes them. They turn away and thank God this didn't happen to them or those they love. Then there are others who see but look straight through Gregory, as though he weren't even there. They speak of anything except the child before them. Again, it is their own pain they avoid facing. Gregory cannot touch these people.

Others, however, dare to look, dare to ask, dare to encounter. These approach nervously at first, but, eventually, love conquers their fear. Gregory's acceptance of their touch, his soft laughter at the sound of their voices, endears him to them. They wonder at his tranquility and peace. In time their original discomfort melts into the same ease the world expresses toward all infants. Self-conscious reserve and detachment, both self-imposed, crumble as Gregory engages them in the primitive banter of early childhood. This eternal infant rules sovereign and welcomes all in his patty-cake, hugs-and-kisses kingdom.

Although my brother's brain is damaged beyond repair, his heart remains uninjured. He is free in ways that I and most others will never be. He is free to love and be loved. That is the "power of the powerless." Gregory is the helpless helper, the injured healer. Gregory is the giver. And I am blessed to be one to receive his precious love.

An Invitation to Listen

(Barry)

"Conversation was never begun at once, or in a hurried manner. No one was quick with a question, no matter how important, and no one was pressed for an answer. A pause giving time for thought was the truly courteous way of beginning and conducting a conversation."

These were the words of a man of the later 1800s, who grew up in a 'natural way' before the age of instant communication and instant distraction: Luther Standing Bear, a "chief," or wiseman to the Lakota peoples. The attitude of which he spoke expressed the only way to truly listen. It was an attitude of respect, the only way to be open to that which Gregory had to offer.

Gregory was one of those kids who often gets shuffled off to a long-term medical care environment. He was profoundly retarded, could not talk, could not crawl, was extremely nearsighted, had a seizure disorder, and was prone to having seasonal viruses develop into pneumonia. Even some in the medical community treated him as a set of numbers on a lab test. The world was all too often not able to or not willing to listen. The thought sometimes occurred to me that it is a wonder that any infant made it beyond the age of six months except for the willingness and innate ability of mothers to listen.

At about seven months of age, Gregory finally succeeded rolling from his back to his front. It was a noteworthy accomplishment that deserved an excited phone call to me at work. We started looking at potential therapies which might help with his initial diagnosis of spastic quadriplegic cerebral palsy.

The first we found was a technique called 'patterning.' It was based on the idea that the ability to walk was the culmination of the proper sequence of steps. An infant first raises its head in response to something of interest, then supports herself up on the elbows and forearms. After that she would start crawling toward the interest, and finally would begin the effort to start walking. A practitioner of this approach would identify what phase needed to be learned anew. Relatives and friends could then assist the person to repeat the phase through constant repetitions. Even if the force of motor movement was coming from an assistant, the brain would eventually learn the proper pattern for the phase. Proponents of this technique claimed some successes, but critics were wary of stories of many hours of forced movement. Sharon and I both had a negative gut reaction towards its use with Gregory. We just filed it away in the back of our minds.

Some time afterwards, we came across a physical therapy technique called the 'Feldenkrais' method. I picked up a book on the subject: *The Illusive Obvious*. Its author, Moshe Feldenkrais, was a physics and judo student, who had suffered a knee injury. Observing his own body mechanics, he became aware that he had developed a new walking pattern to minimize his discomfort. This 'new way' had unconsciously become a habit. Initially it made things feel better, but it kept him from walking properly and, when persisted, caused problems of its own doing.

All forms of physical therapy, by necessity, understand proper body mechanics. Each can point to some notable success stories. In this case it was some adults with cerebral palsy, and sports stars like Julius Ivring of the Philadelphia 76ers, who used the Feldenkrais approach to gain better body control. We felt some hope. Still, I thought how could anyone get Gregory to listen to an instructor?

There was one episode in the book which jumped out to me. It held the kernel of an answer. I perceived it as an invitation to listen. While studying at the Sorbonne in Paris, Moshe decided to take a drawing course. At their first meeting, the art instructor put a white flower vase on top of a white stand. He handed the physics student a piece of charcoal, a piece of moist bread for an eraser, and a drawing pad. The preposterous request was of course, to draw the vase; no instructions, no lessons; just draw the vase. Somewhat flustered, he first drew a small oval for the top, added a curved line for each side and a small swoop for the bottom. As he began to add some shading he was stopped by the art instructor.

"Where on the white vase are there any black lines?"

The instructor then told him to draw what was actually in front of him: areas of white and areas of shading. When the drawing was finished, Moshe stepped back, somewhat amazed. The drawing must have been done by an unknown artist, and not by the man who knew that the top was an oval shape and that sides were lazy 'S' lines. By means of this gentle rebuke, the amazed student was encouraged to listen to what was actually right in front of him instead of his own preconceived notions.

The physics/judo student went on to study body mechanics and to develop his own physical therapy approach. It used gentle assistance techniques; to help the patient listen to the feel of proper body motion which, he suggested, the brain is already wired to accept. In order to do this 'listening', the distractions of unnecessary noise and visual stimulation are minimized. Needless disorder would make it difficult, especially for someone like Gregory, to feel proper order.

The gentle, intelligent approach to physical therapy seemed right for Gregory. Sharon made some calls and found out that a team of therapists who had studied directly under Moshe Feldenkrais were coming in from Israel during the summer to teach his techniques out at Amherst College. The sessions were intended for training of other physical therapists, but they were willing to see Greg during off hours. The cost was rather modest, but it was a three-hour drive each way for a therapy session.

Over the course of six weeks, when Gregory was two years old, we all took one day a week to make the three hour ride out to Amherst College. Usually I drove while Sharon took care of the kids in the back seat. She often made a small picnic for Matt and would read the likes of Mother Goose or Donald Duck so that we all could be entertained.

During most therapy sessions, Sharon would go in alone with Greg. On two of the visits, the therapist, a young woman named Anot, asked me to accompany Gregory. The first time I went in I put Greg down on a cushion covering an exam table while she closed the blinds. Anot took a wooden dowel and held it horizontally a little above his chest until he reached up and grasped it. She would gently move one of his hands and shift the orientation of the dowel until he grabbed it again with both hands. It was interesting to watch the give and take between the two of them. At one point Anot told me, in her broken English, to take the dowel and watched as I quietly imitated her movements. It was easy to get lost in the interplay with Gregory and ignore her. She interrupted a couple of times to have me reposition the dowel. My interactions with Greg seemed to please her.

The improvements in Greg's motion by the end of summer session were noticeable if you were attentive to him. But, starting with fall's cold and virus season, asthmatic reactions, pneumonias, and other medical issues took center stage. In the following year, we found a Feldenkrais therapist more locally, in the outskirts of Boston. He was able to help Greg with some of the tightness in the tendons of his ankles and feet.

In the end however, we found out that the cause of Gregory's physical problems were not due to a static cerebral palsy birth defect but rather to a progressive neurological disorder. No physical therapy, no matter how intelligent and appropriately applied, could serve as a means to overcome his disorder. However, as our experience bore out, the invitation to listen was always a key element at the core of any honest attempt to help him.

Most in the healing arts professions who were good at what they did possessed an innate ability to listen – to the medical data, to Gregory, to Sharon, and to the limits of their own abilities. We gravitated toward the best of these as we found them. Others also had talent and expertise but appeared muted by their own internal noise. One was an orthopedic surgeon we were referred to at a renowned Boston hospital; when we first met him, he examined Greg and mentioned that he could do heel-stretch surgery on Gregory.

"It would improve his ability to bear weight on his feet."

Had he asked first, we could have explained that Gregory had not yet tried to crawl, never mind attempting to bear weight and stand up.

We let his surgical comment slide by. However we did follow his advice to employ temporary casts and special shoes to attempt to straighten out the inward curvature of Greg's feet. At our last follow-up appointment, the surgeon seemed overworked, tired. The improvements in foot curvature were noticeable but small. Gregory still could not put on an ordinary pair of shoes. Examining his patient, he let a small sigh escape referring to Greg as "One of God's little mistakes." I almost felt sorry for the man.

Gregory's quiet invitation did not seek dominion. Words, by their very nature, seek some place of dominion, and are therefore inadequate to describe his quiet. It is far better to present a picture Sharon took at a beach one afternoon when Greg was five. It is a picture of Gregory with Debbie, a 'special ed' teacher, Greg's special friend. It is obvious that she was responding to his quiet invitation. I'm sure that Luther Standing Bear and Anot would agree.

Spring's Colors

The purple hue from the early crocus flower is spring's first sign. Warmer temperatures do battle with the last of winter's snow. The soil thaws, life grows. Lawns turn green. Forsythias splash bright yellows all over the neighborhood. Each new color draws attention, an invitation to focus on its moment, never looking forward or backward in time. By the time tulips make their bright-clustered statements, images of winter's depressing din are nowhere to be found.

And so it was with Gregory. By about the age of two he had filled out a little, became more robust, stronger. Initial surgeries were behind us, and he rebounded from his seasonal hospitalizations with more vigor. In his springtime, memories of vivid color began to dot family life. We lived in the moment, captivated by the glow of each burst of color. Some were associated with things Gregory saw, and some by things he didn't.

Casey

One day we were all sitting down on a blanket in the middle of the living room floor. We propped some pillows around Greg so we could back away and allow him to attempt to maintain his balance. Sharon and I walked over toward the kitchen when Matt's Springer Spaniel, Casey, decided to go over toward Gregory and investigate. Springer's are loveable dogs, excitedly ditsy perhaps, but very desirous of attention.

Casey was usually attentive to Greg's presence. I thought nothing of it when he sniffed Greg's face. When Casey gave him a little lick, I quietly called his name, attempting to divert his attention. But as I turned toward the fridge, a loud yip pierced the house! Evidently Casey returned back to Greg and licked his face. Gregory couldn't see it coming. The dog wouldn't stop, and Gregory reacted by making one of his mad faces. Evidently, he bit down on Casey's tongue and wouldn't let go. Casey started to pull away. I couldn't believe that a dog's tongue was that long! Gregory loosened his biting grip just before I rushed over to him. He was fine. Casey, however, was keeping his distance for the moment. But it wasn't too long before he was lying down near Gregory to keep a protective eye on things. Springers, after all, are love sponges.

The Italian Connection

One day our friend Judy stopped by for a coffee visit with Sharon. Before the kids were born, we lived in an old-fashioned Italian neighborhood in Mansfield, Massachusetts. The families there, including Judy's extended family, often enveloped us in their local festivities. Except for some of the questionable homemade wine from an elderly neighbor, it was an affirming and interesting experience.

Gregory was born after we moved away to our first home. Judy's last two kids, twins, were born near the same time. Sharon and Judy used the same hospital and OBGYN group. One of the twins was born with a cleft palate along with some other physical problems. It was natural to keep up the friendship, helping each other whenever possible.

Judy walked into our home one day, greeting Gregory with the same exuberance she always expressed toward him. She went over to where he was lying on a blanket, bent down, and kissed him on the cheek with one of her flamboyant Italian gestures. Yes, she had heard the story about Casey's tongue, but she had a fondness for Greg and trusted that he returned the feeling. Without looking at Greg's demeanor, she continued on and moved forward to kiss him on the forehead, gesturing and talking to him all the time. Then, all of a sudden, there was a surprisingly loud yell: "Ouch! Greggie!"Judy stood up, holding her hand on her breast, wincing somewhat. She looked down at him and said: "Gregory David; that hurts! Did your daddy teach you to do that?"

It was building up within me. I just couldn't resist. In the proudest, best Italian accent I could muster, I replied, "Atsa my boy!" I caught some guff for the next ten minutes or so, but it was well worth it.

Bright Red

It was obvious that Gregory did not see things well enough to respond to until they were right on top of him. Despite earlier failed attempts to evaluate his vision, Sharon felt strongly that a pair of glasses might be of some help to him. So she took Greg to a local ophthalmologist. He tried to make some measurements while Sharon held Greg in her lap. After the exam, he turned to Sharon and said: "Gregory appears to be extremely nearsighted. As you saw, it was difficult to get reliable measurements, but glasses might be of benefit to him. If you want, I can give him some glasses, but I can't guarantee that they will do much for him."

"How do I tell if they work?" Sharon asked.

"Well, I've worked with kids like this before. If the glasses help Gregory to see more clearly, you should see a noticeable response. You might even have some trouble taking them off of him. It's up to you."

"Okay, let's try them. Just call me when the glasses come in."

In about a week, Sharon got a call from the office receptionist and drove over to get Greg's glasses. Matt and I put Gregory in his wheelchair while waiting for Sharon to return. I was a little doubtful, but Matt seemed excited. On her return, Sharon walked into the kitchen and put the glasses on Gregory. He didn't fuss any, so I cleaned off the kitchen table and put a bright red coke can on it.

Sharon and Matthew were talking softly to Gregory, waiting with quiet anticipation. "Okay, Greggie, everything is fine. Just look at the table."

I slid the can to the edge of the table and slowly began to move his wheelchair closer. When Greg got about a foot from the table, he looked up and stared for second, nose to can. Gregory's face lit up with a wide smile. He threw his head back against the head rest and let out one of his patented belly laughs. We were all smiling when Gregory suddenly lurched forward, almost hitting his head on the edge of the table. I quickly pulled the wheelchair back.

Matt shouted: "Do it again, Dad."

But Sharon quickly stepped in: "Be careful. He almost hit his head!"

"Okay, Mom," Matt replied.

I let Matt slowly push the wheelchair forward this time. Almost on cue, Gregory began laughing again. We all enjoyed this game for a while. Then I picked Greg up and put him on the blanket on the living room floor. He didn't tug at the glasses or attempt to pull them off.

Matt went over and got down right in his brother's face. Greg focused on Matt's face for a while before pulling his hands up by his mouth, clenching each into a tiny fist to make one his 'mad' faces. Matt laughed and chided his brother, "You little stinker!"

The Story

It has been thirteen years since Gregory left us, loosening his earthly bounds. The pain and grief originally came in gargantuan waves, washing each of us out to places of unknown isolation. For each of us, it was within shouting distance of that one place of divine isolation as recorded in Matthew: "Eloi, Eloi, lama sabachthani?" For Sharon, the pain of a devoted grieving mother, it was almost too much to look at. For Matthew, ever his brother's protector, life would present more struggles to hone his strength as he became a clinical therapist, a principal of an inner-city high school for special needs kids with behavior issues, and most importantly a devoted father. For myself, strength and bearing have often been reduced to the effort of putting one foot in front of the other, trying to continue on. I sometimes felt like Schindler after the war, left to my own devices, not knowing where to navigate.

There was, however, one more task for Sharon, Matt, and me: the task of sharing a story of love; the story of the *"helpless helper, the injured healer."* Growing up, Sharon was known as a gifted student and creative writer. However a natural sense of shyness hid her intuitive gift of perspective and her remarkable flow with words. The reality of her inner world remained hidden.

I had assumed that her talents were meant for Gregory's story. As his illness neared its final stages, Sharon reached out to a local parish priest for some help. Father Ron, a Jungian therapist, encouraged Sharon to revive her creative talents to provide expression for what was going on inside. The efforts seemed to be of some help. But after Greg's passing, the pain was too raw for any form of naked expression. She did, however, encourage me to start writing Greg's story, from a father's perspective. At a later point she suggested we could combine our efforts in some complementary form. With Sharon's help, I began the effort and joined a local writer's group.

Leaning on the encouragement from this group, I began the effort to put my perspective about Gregory's story together. I did not consider myself a 'writer' who can craft a good story, who can naturally let the words flow in a compelling manner. It is not my gift. My love for Gregory was, and is, my gift. About six month ago Sharon succumbed to a heart attack, loosening her earthen bounds. She and Gregory are free now, happy again, beyond any measure seen this side of heaven.

It was now clear to me that this was not my story to create in a literary sense. It is mine only as a witness and as a father: a story to narrate. For the story itself was crafted by a divine hand. So, I began my narration with a scene written through Sharon's hand for Father Ron. It is a moving story of The Choice in a 'Divine Race,' a story of truth lived out in our family.

The Choice

(Sharon)

This story starts somewhere on the approach to the finish line, in the present moment, as I live it. I look back briefly at the nineteen-year stretch behind me, catching random memories that settle with the kicked up dust where race horses leave the gate. At a distance, the starting gate stands sturdy in its promise of glory for the elect of the next line-up of racers. The thunderous scramble of hooves is temporarily silenced into a moment of reflection. Nothing is official in this unfinished space and time, until the last, lone contender passes under the checkered flag and stops the clock. Still, I watch the fieldsmen – believing they know the outcome – rake the earth smooth again in anticipation of future runs and victories. The final straggler, near the end of his lap, is merely a technicality. He doesn't really count to anyone but me.

I have placed all my bets, against all odds, on the running of this racehorse. For most, this horse was out of the running on the day he was born. I, however, see something they don't, something beyond the expected and accepted. The knot in my heart grows tighter as his pace becomes more arduous and his breathing deep and labored. Still, he pushes toward the finish with such determination. This young horse is running for his life. That he will place last has no meaning. This is his one and only race, and his persistence will win him honors in a realm where spirit and endurance are valued. All this little horse must do is

100

complete the race and he wins, no matter what his standing in the ordinary world. I watch as the spectators leave the bleachers to find their best vantage point at the winner's circle, even before the official call of the race. What remains my horse's moment of glory will be missed. The crowds can't watch what they perceive and judge as humiliation and defeat. The longshot always loses favor quickly when the clock strikes against him. Losing is intolerable.

No one stands beside me to share these last moments. I sit alone and watch my horse run. With all my inner strength, I muster a cheer, "Be strong, baby. Be strong. You're almost there," knowing that my solitary hurrah holds more magic for him than the roar of any crowd. No one else exists in our world any longer. I understand, somewhere in my heart, that this moment is eternity, that state of being where nothing but love exists. And I wonder, why can't anyone see this but us?

BARRY KRAVITZ is a grandfather with a bent toward the creative; from building a cabin on Maine's sea-coast to coaching a boy's soccer team to being an emergency math/science tutor. His writings include engineering white papers, an award-winning essay on unconditional love and his current effort about a family's remarkable journey with a profoundly handicapped child.

ALABAMA DAWN

Gray steam rises above the gulf
Warm and blue with cold air
Sweeping from the north
White gulls weeping in the
Chill.
Until….the sun slowly rises
With hope of warmth.
Streaking pink and yellow
New day mellow with promise
In Alabama.

REMEMBERING

A father's
Defiant dying in the final stage,
Slipping away
But not fast enough,
Predicted sooner
Yet not soon enough
For him.
Twenty years ago
Yet none too soon
For him.
Not us.

MILES AWAY

Miles away yet near
Enough to touch my life
Then fade away,
Missing all the day to day
Events.
Escape at times to
Closer heat and
Touching you where
I want to be remembered
Miles away.

ENDLESS

Winter rhythms
Winter cold
Wet with bold
Winds and snow.
April teases
With future promises
But winter won't let go.

POWERLESS
(IN BLACK AND WHITE)

Thirty powerless hours and counting on a dark, frozen December night. Forty degrees inside our home, the temperature dropping silent and steady. In the dark and cold, the many layers of flannel not helping much as the minutes and hours pass by in the gloom and bitter freeze…Reflecting shadows from lighted candles with deep snow and ice on the outside deck, along with cartons of milk, ice cream, and orange juice which will be well chilled tonight in the zero degrees. Inside, powerless.

The hours of the night slip by on our street in absolute frozen blackness from house to house. Just visible in the dark from the corner of our side window, one block south on Seatower Road, the red, green, and gold Christmas lights are blinking against the snow, windows full of light and warmth so very close, so colorful in celebration…we are just a few yards away in icy black and silence…powerless.

For Keith

AUGUST FADE

Just a hint of shorter days
Cooler evenings in pink and haze...
Holding on to minutes, days
Which slip away
To colorful and crisp
September ways.

SUDDENLY AT HOME

Lost for a moment
Lost for a while
Gone suddenly in silence.
Escape from the pain
By terrible choice
Leaving misery, guilt, and
The loss of his voice.
Forever.

KATHRYN MARIE GOLDEN was born into a large, loving Irish family in Fall River, Massachusetts. After studying English at Bridgewater State and URI, she moved to Illinois with her husband where she converted to teaching college criminology. Kathryn later returned home to family, friends, the beauty of New England, and the joy of writing.

AFTER HAUL-OUT

Photo credit: Eirian Evans, courtesy of Wikimedia Commons.

Do you ever
just watch?
Plant your eyes on a cloud
that's
frozen
as if reluctant to go,
stretched back on her pillowed couch,
steamy breath signing the air.

It's difficult to reside
only there
as coat finally unthreads
blinking back the last rosehips
which reveal blue mussel flakes –
hard not to peek
nor contemplate
before
she leaves.
Impossible, you may think
To halt your thinking.

‡ ‡ ‡

There are times we look
and wish memory will creep in –
though he flits and dances
close to our reach –
someone calls out
shooting stars from a deck;
two thumping steps perk up the dog,
front door krumps shut;
a supper five years later: young men
grip their mugs,
installers of heating and irrigation,
a budding history teacher, investment manager,
they cajole with caroled barbs
We leave without saying it.

‡ ‡ ‡

Only one trim cloud line is left now
above Cuttyhunk in the south,
her crackling odor
defies obsidian nightfall.

Be still,
don't flicker
away,
be
still.

and I believe
again
in Lost Boys seeking pirates,
hikers point toward October peaks,
dragons' snouts, their jagged teeth
among hoary beach coals,
a little boy bats polished stones into the water,
his boundless life ahead.

Do you ever
just watch,
try to
stop
yourself
from arcing your way back?

She's finally ready to leave
as a heron flies stiffly east,
over the darkening masts
silent
save for clinking halyards
keeping November time.

THE FIXER

The next man in line had folds tumbling from his chin to an oversized grey hoodie streaked with grass stains. Lumpy held a weed wacker missing its protective cover and trimming line.

"What's the matter with this fella?" Terry asked, his eyes scanning the spool at the machine's head. "Having problems threading the line?"

"Yeah," the man said, wrinkling his nose. "I can't seem to get this open. I've checked the operator's manual, but it doesn't tell you anything."

"Those manuals might as well be written in ancient Babylonian," Terry groaned. He turned the head over, considering the plea from the bushy eyebrows before him. "No screws here. Hmmm. I imagine you tried unwinding it – counterclockwise? Usually there's some kind of spring release."

"Yeah. I think so."

Terry lay the shaft against a dark marble counter. The wide girth of the reception desk complemented the foyer's fourteen-foot ceiling, grounded by a patterned black-and-white tile floor. He cupped the bottom of the drum with his left hand. With his right he dialed back the center of the spool, pushing down the spring release.

"It's hung up pretty good on something." He looked at the man. "Is there cutting line wrapped in here?"

"Must be. My son borrowed it last fall and may not have threaded it right." His eyes flicked to the side.

"No matter," Terry said. "Let's see if we can open her up."

He reached deep into the pocket slip of his uniform and grabbed a flathead screwdriver. It was a dark pulpit robe that fell to his boot tops. The robe had royal blue velvet panels running top to bottom, a la Jimmy Swaggart primed to meet a jump-suited Elvis at the Las Vegas Hilton. Each sleeve had black arm shields festooned with insignias of varied trades and artisans – carpenters, blacksmiths, plumbers and tool-and-die makers, even coopers and vintners, clockmakers, bookbinders, and nurserymen. People traveled from three or four counties away, and even from noncontiguous states, to bring him their broken wares.

Maneuvering his arms through the robe, the younger man pried the spool partway open with the flathead and reached for his thinnest needle-nose pliers. He plucked at the fluorescent orange line that was twisted around the cylinder. Pulling and tweaking it enough to get a working grip, he snipped the line here and there, enough finally to untwist the knot and yank out the spent line.

"That oughta do'er." Terry blew back wisps of straw-colored hair that had flung over the side of his lean, pockmarked face. "Next time maybe have your son thread it using the two gaps in the spool, rather than tying it off that way." He pursed his lips to contain a smile.

"I sure will," the older man said. "Can't thank you enough."

"I see you brought more trimming line. Might as well set 'er up while you're here."

Next came a woman in a bright yellow blouse. She squawked at a young girl hauling an old model dehumidifier that nearly reached her shoulders.

"How ya doin' this morning?"

"Terrible. It's getting hot and I don't have a clue how to get this beast running. Light went on for a filter, and I guess I need to drain it," Hurry Up huffed. "Neighbor just gave it to us."

"Does it run at all?"

"Shuts down right away."

"Where you putting it?"

"My bedroom, I hope."

He glanced at the girl, who tugged at one of her pigtails and stuck out a purple tongue.

"Any access to a drain nearby?"

"Don't think so. Bath's across the hall."

Terry came around front, his black robe swishing the desk. He lifted the dehumidifier on to the counter, a fading vanilla Kenmore with mold spots on the grill panel.

"Let's take a look inside first." He took off the grill and unscrewed the display panel, setting it aside. "Ahh, the capacitor's shot. And the display PCB has some issues." He pointed to the circuit board with its labyrinth of components, some dangling loose.

"Mister, why do you wear that funny gown?" Dark lollipop smudges smeared Not-In- School's mouth. She waved a Gummy Bear his way.

Terry straightened into a formal pose. "This uniform, my young dear, was bestowed upon me after years of diligent study, on my matriculation from the Polytechnic Institute of Stained Hands-On Learning. Better known as Fix-It U. Class of '86." He bowed and brushed away another swath of stray hair. "Honorariums gradus duplicare, '91 and '93. Recertifications 2004, 2009, and 2014. Pending further review."

Not-In-School giggled. "I still think that's a strange gown."

"I try to have it cleaned and pressed every spring." Terry swished back around the reception desk. He offered them a drink. On the far side of the counter, a large pitcher of cucumber ice water and a tray with crystal glasses rested beside a vintage desk lamp. He announced that he would return in a few minutes and disappeared into a side vestibule.

"Sure beats the sludge they pass for coffee at the garage," Hurry Up acknowledged.

Terry returned with a coiled length of garden hose in one hand, circuit board gadgetry, a capacitor, and a new air filter. "This'll just take a few minutes," he said, starting on the board.

"What's the hose for?" Mom asked.

"To drain it. We'll attach it to the outlet on the back. Gravity will do the rest. You might run it out a window, or into the bathroom, maybe from whosever room is close enough – your choice." He smiled at the girl with teeth that, while perfectly queued, emitted a coffee-stained sheen.

As they left, she took another cherry Tootsie Roll Pop from beside the lamp.

The line reached almost to the entrance, a gleaming brass-framed revolving door. Sneer had a broken blade on a Milwaukee SAWZALL he somehow couldn't detach. Misty needed help resetting her grandfather's clock. Cubicle Cutthroat's troubleshooting of a wireless router had backfired. Someone brought in a 1957 Hoover vacuum with a crushed power head and missing all its metal extensions. He gave her a spare Bissell Compact Bagless 10091 from the parts room instead.

Terry LaPlante hustled back and forth. He worked alone, other than Maroney, a seventeen-year-old stock boy-cum-apprentice with the breath of a mongoose. Who tried his best but not all that much.

Some assembly required.

A half dozen clients back he caught a familiar look. A prominent hawk-like nose, signature chestnut-and-white-streaked hair falling to the nape of her neck. Frances, who was old enough to be his great-grandmother, scrutinized the oversized windows opening to the avenue. What on earth is she doing here?

Terry assisted the others ahead of her – new couplings for an air compressor, replacing the bridge of an Appalachian dulcimer, the repair of a broken Japanese pottery bowl applying a lacquer dusted with powdered gold (he had trained in the Kintsukuroi tradition, after all) after requisitioning Maroney to bring out the lacquer mix. Routine stuff.

Frances Flamel stood before him a few feet from the counter. She wore a knee-length leopard-print coat and camel hair boots. Her hands held nothing, dangling ebony bracelets.

"My dear Terrance," she rattled, "you're looking well."

"Et tu, Frances," he said, while silently counting off the faces in line. "I haven't had the pleasure in a long time. What's it been, four or five years now?"

"Approximately fifty-two months and seven days, fourteen hours. Give or take."

Her smile was ancient, accenting a long and narrow head not unlike the bleached skull of a large moose.

"What brings you to these parts?" He sized her up quickly, not wanting to be held long by those cobalt eyes. A glare that had stupefied aspiring alchemists and metallurgists for eons. Machinists were known to drop their tools and run.

"Time passes," her voice rattled again. "Yet some things remain the same. Unresolved. Festering. Not reconciled."

"Sounds like you've been listening to Led Zeppelin again." He glanced at his watch. "Live cut or a track from *Physical Graffiti*?"

"You haven't changed," she clucked. A few boot clicks and Frances leaned over the counter. A bit too close for comfort.

"You *know* why I'm here," she whispered. Her breath was dusty in the same way particles rise to the opening of a mine shaft.

"I know that you're *taking* a lot of time." His shoulders straightened beneath the robe. "There are clients behind you, and I'm running low on caffeine. Can we talk somewhere else, after hours?"

"I've got to take off soon. You know how it is. Other protégés to see, southern latitudes to get to. Another Greek text discovered in Botswana needs to be deciphered." She flexed the fingers of one hand, bone-clicking cartilage on bone. Her bracelet shimmered.

"I remember."

"That's good," Frances said, withdrawing her hands. "Don't forget what you need to do. I can see you haven't quite gotten to it yet." She squared herself away from the counter and then looked back at him.

"I won't be so long next time, Terry. Please, do it for yourself."

"I'll try," he heard himself say, watching her disappear through the revolving door.

‡ ‡ ‡

Home was a singlewide trailer on the outskirts of town encased by groaning shifts of trucks climbing the interstate. Veins of rust streaked the modular, but otherwise LaPlante's small yard was tidy. Pink blossoms poked out from several mature Rose of Sharon bushes that buffered him from a neighbor. A small propane grill stood in the trimmed grass.

Terry stretched on a plastic Adirondack chair smoking, his bare feet propped on rock edge of a small fire pit. He faced a spot next to his pickup where he once parked a boat trailer in the gravel driveway. A scratched travel coffee mug was at the ready.

Festering.

"Not quite, lady," he said to himself before taking a final long haul. His fingers flinched as a spasm shot down one arm from his neck. Catching himself, he flicked the spent butt on the ground. From around the hedge snaked a waft of barbecue, ATV Dude revving up round two of the weekend, no doubt. Confirmed by a series of snorts and Girlfriend Raspuff's cackle. Here they go again.

Terry returned inside for something. The latest issue of *Solar Industry*, an Isaac Asimov title due back soon at the library? He couldn't remember which.

The space was a powder dry cocoon. Slivers of light pierced through nearly closed blinds. Suspended nettles of dust pricked his skin as toes scuffed old stains on the shag carpet. His eyes adjusted to the dark, slowly scanning. He fixed on a large tapestry that dominated the wall. It was some fifteen feet long, from the Elizabethan age. A castle above a forest surrounded by an intricate border of menacing gargoyles and coats of arms. He stared into it. The afternoon we found this – actually, it had found us – resting her head on my shoulder. Hints of honey and lavender and finally at peace. A lifetime ago.

He looked around.

Festering? No. More like buried.

Goddamn it, what'd I do with that letter?

Terry pulled up blinds, cracking windows open. He began searching the trailer.

‡ ‡ ‡

"How can I help this morning?"

A slim man in a perfectly fitting Armani navy suit sniffed. He took the same tone with LaPlante as he would querying the concierge at a luxury Bohemian hotel. "Yes. I've got a major issue with my laptop; I don't know how to fend off all of this spam." He straightened one arm of his jacket, brusquely smoothing a minor crease. "Norton Security has failed me again. I brought it to IT at the firm but they were useless. The Apple Store recommended you. Said it might be Russian bots. Perhaps you can assist."

"Sure. I'll try. Can you leave it?" Terry took in the gel-coiffed brown hair. "This may take a little time."

"Oh, no. I need it asap," Entitled-man replied, half speaking through his nose. "My boss is depending on me for this project. And I've never seen such junk in my life. Freezes all my apps. Right wing crackpots unleashed. NRA bigots, neo-Nazi equivocators, trolls everywhere you look. Can you just *imagine* where they all live?"

"Right. I'm glad to help. But there are seven, eight clients behind you, one with a toddler. Can you leave it with me now, or drop back after work?"

"You're kidding me, right?" He rolled his eyes and crossed his arms.

"I'm sorry. That's about the best I can offer you."

"Well, that's not the level of service I was told about. I guess I can…"

"Can you write your login and password on a business card?"

"You expect me to simply…"

"Yes, so I can get to it later today. Now, if you don't mind stepping around to the right side of the counter, sir. My associate Maroney will secure your laptop."

"*Maroney?* Well." He pouted, regarding Terry's sinewy face for the first time, the mass of forearms unencumbered by the pulpit robe as LaPlante leaned over the counter.

Entitled-man was followed by Snap, who preceded Hazy Lazy and Helicopter Mom. Mom was packing a dented MegaScreen Solitaire handheld and assorted water-damaged Xbox One games. On it went all morning. Just before lunch, a large man with a week's growth of beard matching his whiskey-flushed face came to the counter with a five-gallon gas can.

"My problem is the ethanol they put in gas," he barked. "Freaking regulations gone wild!"

"Ahh, what is it exactly you need help with?" Terry didn't bother brushing back another length of hair that had fallen over his eyes.

"Damned mandates is what I need help with. There's a war on gas, a war on the combustion engine. Thank God we've got regime change." His voice had the intemperate quality of a pugnacious talk show host stuck in an echo chamber. "I deal in small engines – riding mowers, landscapers' walk-behinds, snow-throwers, generators. All professional grade, you know. Don't do homeowners – well, maybe a little on the side. I work really hard, built my own business. Six days a week, and often Sundays. Should have stuck with diesel."

"Okay, but what's the issue you've got today?" Terry interjected. "You mentioned ethanol. Yeah, obviously it clogs your filters, injectors, and carburetors. By attracting moisture, it makes those engines run rough – and worse."

"No, but the real problem is the government. Way out of control." He pulled a plug of grease from his beard, wiped it on his work pants. "EPA wants to shut us all down. My state license keeps changing, sixty new pages last year."

"And the ethanol?"

"Bunch of bull. Fuel goes stale by design. Two- and four-cycles lose half their life. Guys like me get screwed, the guys who make this country run. Only ones benefitting are the cartel."

"The what?" Terry's jaw dropped involuntarily. *I need to send this guy away and pee.*

"The Big Three, the enzyme fuel treatment consortium. Sort of like what they tried to do breaking up the banks – see where that got us?"

Hardest Worker Ever squinted an eye at him. "Say, weren't you at the Ethanol Fuel Conditioner Show in Akron last fall? Didn't I see you at the Lucas booth?"

"At the – what?" Terry stepped back. "Mister, I'm not following you. What is it you're asking me to fix?"

"No, you were there. With that jerk from Star Tron." He poked a thick finger across the counter towards Terry. "And the hipster protector regulator. That little rat."

"Sir, you've got it wrong. I did not attend that trade show." His bladder winced. "And I'm not sure you have your facts straight about ethanol. I believe that during, what, the past few decades, the corn belt states pushed to introduce ethanol fuel blends. New market for farmers. Not sure that it's so much EPA-driven."

"You're a part of it, aren't you?" Hardest Worker Ever's chest heaved. One fist clenched. "This is a shooray, ain't it? And you call yourself the Repair It All Wizard?

"We're going to bring you down. We built this land. We're not handing it away."

Terry looked hard at him. "We're done here." He grabbed his keys from a drawer, noticing that, for once, there was no line out the door.

"I'm going to lunch. So I'd appreciate it if you'd take your gas out as you leave."

"Yeah, well, be warned before." He winced bending a knee to pick up the gas can. "Like they say in physicals, for every action, there's another reaction. You're going to get yours."

"Please leave. Now. And that would be physics, Newton's Third Law of Motion, corrupted."

Terry unzipped his robe after the man left. Telling Maroney to take the afternoon off, he flicked off the lights and closed the blinds. The door bolt snapped shut.

As dusk unfolded, LaPlante sat in front of the fire pit, feeding it with wood scraps and small maple logs. The hum of the interstate had become more sporadic. Even an occasional lowing of a passing trailer was a welcomed pulse, keeping beat with the clanks and aromas of neighbors preparing supper.

Sunset had been their best time. She opened to its varied pallets and suspension, letting the day's load disperse like a milkweed cloud on the wind. When his wife Marie was well enough, and for years earlier, she had gently teased him to build a fire or stay out on the water past last light, drifting with the motor cut as the stars emerged. They observed them like children, wondering how to best introduce them to their own.

Terry absorbed the stillness.

He knew it had not been his fault, but he had never forgiven himself. The letter was folded at his side. It was one he might have written earlier, the one thing he had failed to do.

He stood up, his toes pressing into the dewy grass. He read it to Marie for the first time with a natural cadence, in the same rhythm they dreamed in or named constellations together, in the same way they had held each other, crushed by life's vagaries. When he finished reading, he asked her permission to let go. He placed the paper into the fire.

Still standing, he then gave her permission to move on and touch other lives and join with other souls. It was okay for her to let him go.

Terry settled back in his chair lighting a Camel. He nodded towards the west, from where he knew Frances was observing him. With one hand he reached for the pulpit robe, roughly bundled, and tossed it into the pit.

KEN BRACK is the author of two narrative nonfiction books, *Especially For You* and *Closer By The Mile*. He blogs for *Psychology Today* and in 2008 co-founded a nonprofit bereavement center, Hope Floats Healing and Wellness Center, in Kingston, MA. A longtime journalist, Ken has a M.Ed. from Northeastern University and taught high school English in Boston.

THE ANSWER

Prejudice has an ugly face,
    it isn't pretty, it's a disgrace.
We are all sisters and brothers,
    created to love not hate one another.
Beneath our skins and deep within,
    understanding must begin.
Color, race, and shape of eyes,
    matters naught if we are wise.
Look deeply now at one another,
    learn from sister and from brother.
Find the peace and find the love
    that rains upon us from above.
If each of us is to survive
    we as people must decide,
A change of heart and mind to erase
    prejudice from mankind.

THE BRIDGE TO TOMORROW

"Good Lord, what am I doing up here?" I thought, horrified to realize I was standing on a bridge railing ready to jump off into oblivion. My numb and frozen hands clutched the heavy support wires as the wind-driven sleet whipped my long hair into my eyes. I strained looking out into the dark night when a sudden wave of vertigo hit, causing me to involuntarily grab the icy cable to steady myself from falling into the yawning abyss below. I couldn't tell how long I had been up here, but I knew with the clarity of a sane mind I was in mortal danger.

I tried to think of something to ease the terrible pain, but the intensity of my discomfort only seemed to increase as the cold gusts of wind endeavored to knock me off the narrow girder. Wondering how much longer I could hold on to the wire, a thought hit me that I might have to jump after all to end this agony. I'm too numb and stiff with cold to climb down off the bridge that has become my prison. With a sudden sick feeling in the pit of my stomach, I knew I had no one to blame for this predicament but myself, so with a heavy heart I resigned to whatever fate decreed.

I shouldn't have stopped at that bar on my way home today, but being fired from my job this morning was the last straw in a long list of personal failures. My wife, Marie, had finally had enough of my bitter complaining, nasty attitude, and grumpy behavior, and had informed me before I left for work today that she was taking Joey and Patty to her mother's home in Pelham, New York for a while. She told me she needed some time to think about the future of our marriage and I didn't plead with her to stay. I just grabbed my briefcase and walked out the door.

Later, after getting to work, I screamed at my secretary, Miss Felton, to get me some black coffee and be quick about it. Then I got on the phone with my boss, Mr. Clark, and made up an excuse why the Denton report would be late. There was a long pause, and Mr. Clark asked me to stop into his office for a moment. When I entered the room he asked me to sit down. I told him I preferred to stand and that I hoped this wouldn't take too long because I had a lot of work to do. He sat looking at me with a stern face, and after clearing his throat he said, "I'm sorry Frank, but I find that your work has been inferior for far too long; your attitude has been impossible, and your treatment of your fellow workers has been disgraceful. The only reason I have tolerated your behavior was because of your wife and children." I was stunned, and without saying a word, I turned and left the room.

"Imagine the colossal gall of that man," I raged at Miss Felton. "Clark just fired me! Can you believe that?" Miss Felton sat there speechless. I continued on ranting, "That pompous jerk just fired me. Who does he think he is? Where's the gratitude for all the business I've brought into this company? Where is his understanding that I've had to work with a bunch of incompetent idiots? What about all the overtime I've given this company over the years? The nerve of him firing me. I just can't believe it," I said as I stalked into my office slamming the door.

After cooling down a bit, I asked Miss Felton, on the intercom, to bring me a cardboard box. It seemed ironic, that after working here for over twelve years, all I carried away from the job only filled half the container. You'd think for that length of time the box should have been over-flowing, but I didn't have the usual stuff the other guys had cluttering up their desks and walls, such as family pictures of the wife and kiddies, sports memorabilia, certificates of merit, etc. I couldn't be bothered. Finally, taking one last look at the room where I'd spent so much of my life, I picked up the carton, closed the door, and left without saying goodbye to anyone.

I drove around in my car for a while, trying to get a grasp on what had just happened. There wasn't any sense in going home to an empty apartment. Marie and the kids had gone by now, and who knew when they would be back again, if ever. Then, I drove past Nemo's Bar and decided to turn around for a brew. One beer turned into two, then three, and finally I spent the rest of the day whiling away the time drinking. I felt sorry for myself, and I was carrying a colossal grudge against everyone and everything in my life.

As I hung from the girder, I was filled with anguish, but I was also beyond feeling the cold anymore. I had earned everything that was about to happen to me. I had been a selfish man, a terrible father, and I had treated my friends, neighbors, and co-workers with contempt. I had walked over everyone to get where I was, and look where it has brought me. I started to sob uncontrollably, and thought about all the heartache I had caused the people that I loved. I truly loved my family, but had I ever shown them love? When they find my body, will they feel any pain or sorrow, or will they just feel a sense of relief that I'm no longer around? I can't even leave a note explaining why I had wanted to kill myself. It has always been about me, and I deserve it, and they will hate me for it.

"Oh, God, please forgive me for being an arrogant fool." I continued to cry into the frigid gale. "Please help me! Let me have another chance to do it right. I don't want to die. I want to do things differently and be the man I should have been. I'll be grateful and help others. I'll be a loving husband and father, and I'll apologize to Mr. Clark, and I'll ask for forgiveness from everyone I mistreated at work. Please, Lord, if it be your will; send someone soon to help me get down off this bridge." Hanging my head in shame, I knew one way or another it would be over shortly for it was out of my hands. The wind seemed to strengthen, and howled and swirled as I weakened and my legs started to sag beneath me.

Suddenly, I thought I heard a voice calling out to me from below. Then I heard it again. "Hey Mister!" the voice yelled over the wind. "What do you think you're doing up there? Nothing can be bad enough to drive you to do this. Don't you realize that jumping is a permanent solution to a temporary problem? Give yourself a break fella, and try to work out your problems tomorrow. What do you say pal?"

Helplessly, I nodded my head, for I had no voice left to answer him.

"Okay, Buddy, I'll climb up and help you down. Here take my hand.

Let go of the cable and trust me. Careful now, don't slip. Steady, you're almost there," the man said with emotion.

When my feet finally reached solid ground, I felt my rescuer's strong arms encircle my exhausted body and he half-carried me to his truck and helped me inside. Then he tucked a warm blanket around me, and said, "Let's go get a big cup of hot coffee to help thaw you out. By the way, my name is David. David Browne, and it's good to meet you."

"My name is Frank Westfield," I said through chattering teeth. "I'm glad to meet you, too. Boy, am I ever glad you came. You're a lifesaver, and God bless you. I had too much to drink earlier and did a stupid thing. I must have been out of my mind when I climbed up on that bridge. You were the answer to my prayers. I couldn't have gotten down without your help. Thank you again. Tell me, David, what made you stop, anyway?"

"Well, Frank, I was driving to Chelsea to visit my mother. She hasn't been feeling well lately, so I was going to check on her to see if she needed anything. Then the strangest thing happened. It was as if a voice in my head told me to stop, but I ignored it at first. Then, it told me to back up, and then it told me to stop right here. I got out of my truck and looked around, but I didn't see anything. I was just getting back into the cab, and then I heard the voice again, telling me to look up on the other side. Sure enough, that's when I spotted you hanging onto the wire. Don't ask me who or what made me stop and look up, but I knew something unusual was happening."

"I know who it was," I said as tears began running down my face. "I prayed to God for help, and he sent you to rescue me. I guess I have a great many bridges to mend, starting tonight. Thank you, David, and thank you, Lord, for this chance to rebuild my life and make amends to my wife, children, and friends for all the pain I've caused them. I hope they will forgive me. I know one thing, David; I'll never forget you or this: the worst and best night of my life."

THE DEATH SENTENCE

Doctor Ferguson, the oncologist, told Joan she was terminally ill.
Today she immediately had to start radiation and chemotherapy.
The nausea and vomiting made her so sick.
She thought she was going to die.
She wasn't ready to give up.
The struggle was very hard.
She wanted to live.
Not to die.
She won.
Life!

THE PROMISE

You could cut the silence with a knife, the darkness, too, as I lay in my bed in a fetal position. All I can think about are Arthur's last words to me as he slammed the door and left our apartment.

"Ruthanne, I promise if you ever leave me, I'll find you and I'll kill you."

I knew he meant what he said, but I had to leave. I couldn't bear another minute in this hateful and destructive relationship. Tonight was the last time he would ever hurt me. Usually he hit me where it wouldn't show, so I could go to work the next day. But this time he had hit my face. I had a black eye and a cut on my upper lip. My eye was swollen shut, and my lip was still bleeding, even after putting ice on it. Later he would apologize and say he'd never do it again, but enough is enough.

In the morning, before Arthur returned home from work, I'd be gone. I had it all planned out. A cab was coming to pick me up at five A.M. My bag is packed, the money is in my purse, and I have a safe destination in mind. If he comes home early, I'm going to kill him. At least I'll try, I hate him enough, and it would be self-defense.

The syringe is waiting under my pillow. I had taken it from the hospital lab where I work. It gives me comfort knowing I can fight back the next time I become a victim. Hate can make a person do what they never think they are capable of doing.

It wasn't always like this. In the beginning, two years ago, when we first met, Arthur was kind, thoughtful, and loving, but he was insecure and possessive. Soon he alienated my family and friends and had to know where I was every minute, and then he began to hurt me. I would have left sooner, but I was afraid. Arthur has destroyed my love for him.

Wait! I hear something. Oh no! He's coming back. I can hear his key turning in the lock. Slowly, I reach under my pillow, pull out the syringe, and uncap it. It is filled with a fast-acting sedative that is difficult to detect. If he touches me again, I'll stab him with it, and then I will be free. My hand is steady, I'm not afraid anymore. He's standing beside the bed, and I can hear him breathing. His hand touches my shoulder. He says, "I'm sorry Ruthanne," but it is too late. I jab the needle into his thigh and press the plunger with my thumb. He screams.

"Why did you do that to me? I came to say I was sorry." His body hits the floor with a loud thud as he struggles to breathe. I lay there in my bed until there is silence. Sorry, Arthur. Apology not accepted.

THE PROPOSAL

Tonight Justin is coming to pop the question. The dining room is warm and inviting, and the table gleams in the candlelight. The aromas wafting from the kitchen are delectable, but I am nervous as I await his arrival. He called yesterday to say he had a special question to ask me when he comes for dinner tonight.

Promptly at eight o'clock the doorbell rings, and Justin is finally here.

"Hi Sweetheart, you look great," he says as I open the door. Then he notices the dinner table.

"Shelly, what's going on here? What's the big occasion?"

"That's for you to say, Justin," I reply coyly. "So, come sit down, dinner is already."

"Well, this is certainly nice. You've never gone to this extreme before."

"Special occasions deserve a beautiful dinner, don't you agree?" And food is the way to a man's heart, I thought.

"Wow, roast chicken, mashed potatoes with gravy, green peas, and pearl onions –all my favorites. This is wonderful. And cranberry sauce, too. Oh, I love it."

"I'm glad you like it," I purred.

"I don't know what I did to deserve this, Sweetheart, but thank you," he said wiping gravy off his chin.

I served the dessert, apple pie ala mode, Justin's favorite, and waited, and waited.

Finally, I couldn't resist, so I asked, "Justin wasn't there a question you wanted to ask me tonight?"

"Oh yeah, there was, but it can wait. I'm really enjoying this pie. Did you make it yourself?"

"Of course I did. I made the whole dinner."

"Shelly, if you keep on cooking like this, you'll make someone a happy man someday."

"Justin, I love making you happy."

"Oh, Sweetheart, if you think I was going to ask you to marry me, I wasn't."

"You weren't?"

"No, I was going to ask you to babysit my dog Fritz, that's all."

"Let me get this straight, Justin. All you wanted was for me to babysit your dog?"

"Right, Shelly, we've been good friends for years, but I'm not ready to get married to you, or anyone else for that matter."

"You're right, Justin. We've seen each other every weekend for years. We go to the movies, or bowling, or we go out to dinner! All along I've thought we were dating and that you loved me!"

"I do, but not enough to get married."

"Get out, Justin!"

"I'm sorry to disappoint you, Shelly."

"Just leave."

"It really was a great dinner."

"Go, Justin."

"Okay, okay, I'm going. By the way, Shelly, is it still on for watching Fritz next week?"

TO SNOW OR NOT TO SNOW

As I looked out my kitchen window
I wasn't filled with woe
The landscape was withered and brown
But no longer covered with snow
In early winter at the first sight
I viewed the snow with such delight
Its beauty so calm and serene
It made such a lovely scene
But alas it snowed every other day
And I yearned for it all to go away
The snow continued into April this year
And I began to worry and to fear
When would it ever just disappear?
Then came the joyful day
Most of the snow had melted away
All that remained was in the hedges
In the bushes and around the edges
No longer beautiful and serene
No longer clean and pristine
What was left was covered in dirt
And that's why I call the old snow snirt.

WICKED DECEPTION

My eyes are glued to the clock as I wait for my lover to come and kill my husband. Howard and I went to bed early tonight, but I can't sleep. I'm here lying beside the man I've been married to for twenty years and soon he'll be dead. I don't feel anything except relief, because I'll soon be free.

You may wonder how I arrived at this point in my life. As I think back, it was a particularly restless and boring day when I happened to meet Jake. What can I say? He was trouble looking for a place to happen, and that's when he caught my eye. I had gone shopping but couldn't find anything interesting. Buying things usually got me over one of these moods, but not that day.

It was too early to go home, so I stopped at a nearby lounge for a mid-afternoon pick-me-up. Sitting in the dimly lit bar, a man was staring at me. He raised his glass, smiled, and nodded his head as if to ask permission to join me at my table. Without giving it a thought, I nodded back. That's how I ended up having an affair with Jake Mills.

Now here I am, sitting in my den, waiting for a police lieutenant to tell me if my husband is dead or alive, and all I can think about is Jake.

‡ ‡ ‡

Jake is handsome in a dark, mysterious way. His brown eyes had held me mesmerized as he told me about himself that afternoon. He was a Harvard graduate, a business entrepreneur, and very wealthy, and I was smitten before the first drink was finished. I found out later that none of it was true, but at that time, he was all that was missing in my life. Excitement, mystery, and passion – that was Jake, and I wanted more.

Jake was thirty-five and younger than me. At forty-two I didn't care, especially when everyone said I didn't look my age. When he asked me, I fudged a little and took off five years. A three-year difference didn't seem so bad, and we really hit it off right from the beginning.

Time passed quickly, and Jake and I met every chance we could. At first I believed his excuses for his small apartment. He said his penthouse was being remodeled, and he had to live there for the time being.

To be on the safe side, I hired a detective to check into his background. He told me that Jake was a scam artist. He picked up wealthy women for a living and romanced them until they wised up, but I knew Jake and I were different. He told me he wished he had met me years ago and that I was the only woman he had ever truly loved. All the others had meant nothing to him.

The final proof of his love was he never took any money or gifts. Once, when I bought him a Rolex watch for his birthday, he said it was too expensive and to take it back. I'd had it engraved with the date and 'All My Love, Jackie'; I insisted he keep it. Finally, he reluctantly, accepted it.

After a month, I wanted out of my marriage to Howard. I loved Jake so much, but I had signed a pre-nuptial agreement and I didn't want to lose my current lifestyle. Howard had a large insurance policy, and I was his sole beneficiary. If something happened to him, I'd be set for life, so the only solution was to get rid of him.

You should know about the first night I met Howard Winthrop. I knew right away he was going places because he was very intelligent. He wasn't handsome, but he had nice eyes and smile, and after a few dates my mother told me I should snap him up quickly before someone else did.

"But, Mom," I told her, "I don't love him."

She had replied, "Jackie that doesn't matter. His father is wealthy, and he owns a big company. Someday it will be Howard's, and he can give you a good life. You may not love him now, but that can follow later. It's just as easy to love a rich man as a poor one," was her motto. So in our senior year of college we became engaged and were married right after graduation.

I settled for the good life, but not for love, and not having children was probably a big mistake. It might have made a difference, but Howard didn't want a family. He said, "Kids are noisy, messy, and a lot of hard work," and I'd lose my figure, and that would be a shame. He worked long hours and took over the company when his father passed away a few years later.

I tried to fill the emptiness with volunteer work at a nearby hospital and playing bridge with my friends. I took up tennis and swam in the pool at the country club, but it wasn't enough. There wasn't any fun, joy, or laughter between us, and I always wondered why he had married me. Probably he did it to make himself look good with a pretty woman on his arm. I know it sounds shallow and cold, but I guess we both got what we wanted. Consequently, we were two not-very-nice people.

‡ ‡ ‡

Two weeks ago, after a particularly romantic interlude, Jake said, "Jackie, it's too bad you can't divorce dear old Howard. We'd be free to leave Boston. We could travel, you know, maybe take a cruise. I'd even marry you if you were free, so what do you think?"

"Jake, if I dumped Howard, I'd be broke in six months. That pre nup I signed twenty years ago is only for two hundred thousand dollars. I like having a nice house and all that goes with it, so what's the solution?"

The question hung heavy in the air between us as we both looked at each other, knowing the answer.

‡ ‡ ‡

Now it's almost twelve o'clock, and Jake will be here any minute. He has a gun, and he'll come into the house and fix the problem.

I felt Howard move beside me. He touched my shoulder and whispered, "Jackie! Wake up. I heard a noise. I think there's someone downstairs."

"Come on, you're just dreaming."

"No, I'm not. I heard a thump."

"Well I don't hear anything," I grumbled. "You woke me up just to tell me that?"

"Wait a minute. There it is again. Didn't you hear it? Somebody is walking around down there and bumping into the furniture."

"Okay, Howard, you're right. I hear something."

"I'll go down and check it out, but you stay here," he said fumbling around in the drawer of the nightstand.

"What the heck are you doing?" I hissed in impatience.

"I'm trying to find the gun and the damn flashlight. Here they are. I'll be right back."

"Hey, I want to come too."

"Don't argue with me, Jackie; it's not safe. I'll call you when it's all clear."

"All right, but be careful. He might have a gun too, you know."

He left me sitting in the dark, waiting for his call, and I'm terrified something will go wrong. Wait a minute: I hear voices. Howard is yelling. He's demanding that someone turn around or he'll shoot. All of a sudden, two shots ring out, shattering the stillness of the night. I spring out of bed and tiptoe to the top of the stairs. I can't hear anything below, so I call out Howard's name.

"Howard, are you all right?" There's no answer, so I start down the stairs, stopping every few steps to listen. There's no moaning or heavy breathing, just the loud thumping of my heart in my ears. Step by step, I edge into the living room, and then I trip over something on the floor. I drop to my knees and I feel around. It's a body, but I can't make out who it is and I'm too frightened to turn on the lights. I wait, kneeling on the floor, trying to think of what to do. I hear heavy footsteps out on the porch, then the doorbell rings, and someone is banging on the front door.

I scramble to my feet and rush to open it, but I'm all fingers and thumbs as I fumble with the lock and chain. When the door swings open, a policeman is standing there holding a flashlight in my face.

"I'm Lieutenant Peters, and this is Officer Burns," he said. "A neighbor called 911 and reported gunshots. What's going on here?"

"I don't know, my husband and I heard noises, and he went down to see what was happening. Then I heard the gunshots. I came down and found a body on the floor. Oh no, I don't feel so good. I think I'm going to be sick to my stomach," I said, starting to sag at the knees.

Peters grabbed me and shouted to Burns, "Get the lights," and he carried me into the den and put me on the sofa. I pretended to pass out, and he left me there.

After a while, I got up and headed for the living room. When I entered, the body on the floor was covered with a white sheet and Lieutenant Peters was busy talking to a technician. I didn't care if I was interrupting him.

"Lieutenant," I demanded, "who is this," I asked, pointing toward the body on the floor. "Is it my husband?"

"Mrs. Winthrop, please go back to the other room. I'll be right with you and explain everything," he said with firmness.

"But Lieutenant, is that my husband or isn't it? I have a right to know. Why are you treating me this way? If you don't tell me right now, I'll take this up with the police commissioner, who is a good friend of mine."

"Okay Mrs. Winthrop, I guess I'm finished here for now, so why don't we both go back to the den, and I'll bring you up to date on what we know so far."

"It's about time, Lieutenant. I'm worried about my husband."

"He's busy in the kitchen talking to one of my men," Peter's said.

"You mean he's still alive?" and I started to sob.

"Yes Mrs. Winthrop. I know you're crying in relief, but I assure you he's fine."

"Lieutenant, if Howard is alive, who is that in the other room on the floor?"

As I asked the question, the horrible truth was apparent. It was Jake lying there, and Howard was alive. That wasn't supposed to happen. I had taken the bullets out of his gun earlier that evening. When did he put them back in? Jake didn't have a chance. My mind is reeling, and I have to pretend I'm relieved my husband is alive. All I can hear is the lieutenant's voice babbling on in the background saying, "We're not sure yet, Mrs. Winthrop, but a tentative ID has been made from the identification card in his wallet. We're checking his fingerprints in the IAFIS System right now to see if it's correct. If he has a prior criminal record, we'll know it immediately. There's been quite a few break in's in the area lately, and this guy's probably the one. All we can do is wait for the confirmation."

I pull myself together and wipe my tears from my face, and ask, "When can I see my husband?"

"Not yet. We're not through questioning him. When we're done, you'll see him. Now, do as I say, and stay here," he said as he turned and left the room.

There wasn't anything else I could do, but try to be patient. My heart is breaking, and I want to scream, throw furniture, and tear my clothes in grief. My lover is on the floor under the white sheet, and Howard killed him. He didn't even like guns. He only bought it because of the robberies in the neighborhood, and he had never used it before.

I hear Howard's voice as he's coming down the hallway to the den. Still dressed in his pajamas, he enters the room, and I immediately see he has Jake's Rolex watch on his wrist. Howard notices me looking at the watch and a slight inscrutable smile plays over his lips as he returns my glance.

I can't believe he took it off Jake's body after he shot him, but wait a minute. What's that he's saying to Lieutenant Peters?

"Thank heavens, Lieutenant; I checked the gun before I went to bed. There weren't any bullets in it. Funny thing is I don't remember taking them out. I must have forgotten to put them back in the last time I cleaned the gun," he said as he gave me a knowing stare. "If I hadn't checked it, the outcome could have been a lot different. Wouldn't it, Jackie? I'd be dead, and you'd be a widow now, but we were very lucky tonight. Don't you agree, Dear?"

NANCY WINROTH GAY is a wife, mother, grandmother, and  great grandmother. She has been writing memoir, short stories, poetry, and fiction for eighteen years. She has been published in three anthologies and in the newspaper. She also enjoys reading, completing crossword puzzles, sewing, crafting, painting, and creating jewelry.

ADVENTURE IN A TRIANGLE

These teens know each other well – I'm the narrator – but it's their
story to tell
You are now entering the Bridgewater Triangle

Lake Nippenicket is well known as being part of the legendary
Bridgewater Triangle. The triangular-shaped area extends for 200
miles around Southeastern Massachusetts and is widely recognized for
harboring unexplained phenomena, including giant birds and snakes,
killer dogs, poltergeists, flying creatures, and more. Even UFO and
Bigfoot sightings have been reported. But that never scared us! We had
been water skiing on the lake for years and had never seen anything
that made us scream and run until today…………

A boat ride to the far side of the lake
A familiar old building has lost its shape
Demolished we figured – the foundation in view
Curious kids with a story for you
Furiously running over – a big hole in the ground
Never imagined a huge creature inside waiting to be found

"Come see this humongous thing stuck in the foundation with no
place to go."

"It must weigh about 60 pounds."

"It's not moving."

"It's huge and has an ugly shell."

"Maybe it has been in a big battle, but don't see any blood or guts
hanging out."

"It's super gross looking, can't tell if it's dead or alive."

"Hey, bet it's one of those flying creatures they say live here"

"Remember the documentary we saw about the Bridgewater
triangle?"

"Yeah, with all that weird stuff about lake monsters living here that we never believed? "

"This must be one of them and maybe it has wings so it can fly out of the hole and get us!"

"What should we do?"

A closer look – a minute to calm down

Turtle like and massive – at least 50 pounds

A huge shell alright – dried out, scaly looking for real

Dehydrated and exhausted from its ordeal

"Check it out, there was just a slight movement at the edge of its shell, bet it's still alive!"

"What should we do now?"

"Do we dare try to get it out or should we just let it rot there?"

We all decide that a plan must be made –

some way to work together for its life to be saved

A massive snapper and maybe could fly –

and who's the kid to go inside?

"There must be a big jaw under the creature's dried out shell."

"Will it run if it gets scared, will it fly, will it bite, can it kill us?"

"Will it chase us across the foundation once someone is hoisted down?"

"How can we get away quickly if it decides to attack?"

"How are we going to do this?"

"Who's going to be the one to go into the hole alone?"

One of the boys - thin, agile, and quick –

volunteered for the task

We figured out some rescue details –

will the creature be able to last?

"Let's test it with a long tree limb from above to see if it moves or attacks."

141

"First, spray some water on and under its shell."

"It's not moving – maybe it's too tired or it's dead!"

"Just keep trying."

"Yeah, but let's not become a legend about a bunch of kids lost in the Bridgewater Triangle."

"Stop worrying about creatures and monsters, follow our plan, and save this guy."

"A blanket used as a sling might work to get it out."

"Right, and a sturdy plank to drag it up the eight-foot foundation."

"How are we going to get it into the blanket – like it will just roll into it?"

"How will the rescuer get out quickly if the creature becomes crazy or can fly?"

"We need to find a rope to put in place as an escape route if needed."

Lots to think about in making this plan
The rescuer can climb like a monkey if he's in a jam
Around the torn-down building we found the plank we need
A rope from the boat will serve us well indeed
The creature still in its corner – remaining still
A few more squirts of water for its trip up the planked hill

"How are you going to get the blanket under him? He's too big and heavy."

"Don't get too close – it might be fooling us and playing dead"

"I learned that in science class, how animals play dead sometimes."

"Hey, let's try pushing it a little with a piece of wood and slowly move it into the middle."

"No, the blanket is too scruffy – we need something smooth."

"Oh, that piece of plastic that's in the boat – then put some water on it so it'll slide easily."

"Okay. We Got Him – Success – Time to Cheer!"

Up the plank it went with all hands on board
The lake 20' feet away – we were heading toward
A few more squirts of water to help it ahead
All hoping that the creature was not yet dead

"Do you think it's still alive?"
"It hasn't moved at all – maybe we were just too late."
"Yeah, but at least we made a plan and tried our best."
"All that Boy Scout stuff we learned about teamwork and
brainstorming really helped today."

Slowly carrying the creature in the sling to the water's edge
Submerging it in the water, but was it now dead?
The creature remained quiet and motionless as our excitement turned to dread
It may be time for a tear to be shed

"It's just a big shell and nothing happening."
"Hey, keep going anyway."
"We had a great plan – even a giant creature with wings didn't stop
us."
"Let's just leave it in the water where it belongs."
"Or we could use one of our Scout recipes and make a soup – a
turtle soup."
"That's not funny dude!"

A few splashes of water once into the lake
Some movement under the shell – maybe not too late
Watching in amazement a few strokes and off it went
A day to remember and quite an event.

"Can't believe he made it – he's going on his way."
"Let's come back to the lake soon and see what else we can find."

This story from inside the Bridgewater Triangle – all very true
We're all so happy we could share it with you.

BYE-BYE BUTTERFLY

My kitty so curious from window to window – What does she see?
Another kitty outside acting playful and free
Paws flying around while kitty enjoys fun
Looks like there's little movement from a capture soon to be won
A huge butterfly of yellow and black about two inches in size
Oh, beautiful butterfly – I pray not for your demise
Amazed at how quickly playtime is over
For butterfly who was flying toward a green field of clover
Butterfly so lovely, I wish you could stay
But the call of the wild just ended your day
For me, so sad you won't be going on your way
For kitty, so happy for a moment at play

FOR JUDY, MY DEAR FRIEND

You loved embracing each day to bring all that was good
Always ready to help others and give all that you could
Your life's work was with disabled children, whatever their need
You loved them, and they you, and did much to help them succeed
You kindly touched the lives of everyone you knew
I am grateful your compassion for others – you shared with me too
Your friendship helped me to discover a new direction
The mantra band bracelet you gave me, inspired reaching that connection
Your husband and family were to you most important
Your love for them relentless amid precious time being shortened
You told stories of how much joy your parents brought you in life
You looked forward to being with them again when your dear Lord
     deemed the time right
You had no fear of leaving this world you said, with a quiet smile
The 23rd Psalm had forever been your guide
A slowing of late I noticed with dismay
Still hopes of sunny days and more chats together on the way
Your leaving seemed arriving, although we all objected
Your fine work here soon to be done and this must be accepted
You said good-bye to us on a Saturday night
Your dear Lord and Mother Mary came for you, as the time was right
Your life was one of service to others your family did say
Your spirit of love will forever remain your legacy
I think of you often remembering the laughter and fun
And treasured memories of your amazing love – freely shared with
     everyone

GUESS WHO?

I was sixteen years old at the time, in high school, and thrilled to have recently gotten my driver's license. The day was beautiful and warm, and it was autumn. Too beautiful a day to be in class, but attendance was always a must in my family. It seemed as though the day just dragged on and on, one class after another, until the familiar crackling sound of the PA system brought the afternoon announcements and then the much-awaited dismissal bell. Finally, at last, the school day was done!

I was very excited because my dad worked at the school and now, if he agreed, I would be able to take his car for an afternoon spin. His car was called a DKW and was a German model with a 4-speed shift on the column. I had driven it during my driving test at the registry, so I was familiar with its operation. It looked somewhat like a Volkswagen Bug from the 1950s but was not nearly as elegant. Anyway, wheels were wheels in those days!

When I arrived, Dad was in his office area. He was the head custodian at my school as well as the truant officer. Needless to say, my attendance was quite pristine. I saw him kicking his foot behind a small, fluffy, gray and white kitten trying to get her out the back door. He complained that the kitten had been hanging around all day and that he was annoyed she had made her way back into the school once again. The back door had to remain open for deliveries, so the battle of wills had been going on for hours. Because he liked animals, I knew he would never hurt her and just wanted her to go on her way. So out she went!

We chatted for a couple of minutes about my delightful day at school and then came the big question! "Can I take your car to meet some friends uptown for burgers and fries?" We always went to a local restaurant in the center of town called Larry's. They had the best cheeseburgers ever and the place was packed with high school kids every day after school. He agreed and gave me the keys with strict instructions as to when I should return with the car. Dad was a former Marine, so I knew that his orders must be followed, especially if I wanted to use the car again. He said, 1600 hours. (I had learned the meaning of military time early in life, so 4 P.M. was the deadline.) As I turned to leave, we spotted the little gray-and-white kitten heading back into the school. He told her, in no uncertain terms, to go away and stay away as he motioned to help her along. Again, out she went!

As I walked to the adjoining parking lot to take the car, guess who was in the grassy area next to the walkway? You guessed it, the little, gray-and-white kitten. During my quest for the car, I hadn't noticed how adorable she was and that she was so pretty that she must be a girl. She looked very lost and scared too. Then I had an amazing idea!

We – Mom, Dad, and I – had always had several cats when I was younger. We even had a few dogs, a couple of parakeets, and a turtle in the past, but we had no animals now. My mom, Lois, was an animal lover and I thought, *I'll just scoop this little kitten up and take her home on my way uptown. She can even ride shotgun! It's the perfect time for another kitty anyway, and I'm sure my mom, a wonderful home-maker and caring woman, will just love her.*

As I brought her into the house, mom looked so surprised. I told her the story of how Dad had kept kicking her out of the school all day, telling her not to come back. It was love at first sight for mom as she took the kitten from my arms, cuddled her gently, and said, "She won't be kicked out again!"

Now I had to rush to grab a quick burger with friends and still meet the 1600 hours deadline. I returned the car right on time, keeping the fate of the little kitten a secret.

When Dad arrived home for dinner that night, we greeted him and we all walked into the living room where *guess who* was curled up, sleeping in Dad's favorite chair? You're right again: the little gray-and-white kitten.

Dad exclaimed, "Oh, no – not that cat again. Out she will go!"

But Mom replied, "No, Andy, she will be staying here!"

Shaking his head along with a faint smile, he looked at us and said, "Okay." And that she did!

Guess who was our one and only kitty to be happy, healthy, adored, and loved for sixteen years to come? You got it right again, our little fluffy, gray-and-white kitten. She grew to be a beautiful angora cat who might sometimes be seen at night curled up with Dad in his favorite chair.

We named her Candy – She was always very sweet!

LETTING GO

To let you go after all these years finds a shattered heart surrounded
by a waterfall of tears
A final moment with you and me again by the sea
So peaceful and tranquil – can this really be?
You were my captain and I was your mate – our love discovered in a
moment of fate
Voices whispered, "Their love will never last"
Just a few people talkin' – long lost in the past
I sang to you our favorite song in one-part harmony
Never knowing a northeast gust of wind would quickly return you to
me
Your ashes released – some rushing back into my face like a last kiss
to be
As I set you free to remain forever with your beloved sea

MY MIMI AND GRAMPA

Always together my pair of grandparents you would see
A delightful couple who shared a lot of time with me
Always joy on every occasion with more to come
Each trip ending with a piece of Juicy Fruit Gum
Whether to Old Silver Beach for some fun in the huge waves
Or a trip to a restaurant to sample the pick of the day
Most fun about the two was that they played piano together while
singing as a duet
And Grampa would get up from the piano to dance a soft-shoe no one
could forget
Then, well into their seventies and never missing a beat
My grandparents were a couple everyone wanted to meet
They were so fun and special and I still remember well
My much loved and adored Mimi and Grampa
And there are many more stories to tell

OUR GARDEN

Each summer a huge garden adorned our backyard
All you can imagine from corn and tomatoes, cukes, and chard
The caretaker was my gramps who had a mega green thumb
His garden would flourish every year and he would save everyone some
Great food to eat and enjoy or just bring home
Not far from his garden did my gramps ever roam
He had the gift of giving and always would say
There's plenty for everyone and I enjoy giving some away

A SUMMERTIME FAVORITE

Sitting on my front porch is a summer time best
To relax, meditate, or search the trees for a nest
Sometimes joined by a critter or two
With names like Chip, Chuck, Bunny, or Birdie Blue
Amazing nature to watch and enjoy with a smile
I love my porch, especially in summer
Think I'll sit for a while

 **ROYANN CHARON** earned a M.Ed from Bridgewater State University, a BLS from Mount Ida College, and worked for many years teaching and working with special education students.

She loves the wonderful community and tranquility of living in Bridgewater where she enjoys family and friends, reading, writing, music, yoga, photography, nature, theater, movies, and great fun as a TaleSpinner.

HURL

What a nice surprise! We celebrate with a drink. But my good cheer doesn't last long. The next few weeks are the beginning of hell. I am working, but most days I'm so ill my supervisor doesn't come in my office to say hello and check in as she can hear me retching in my private bathroom. I try everything. Can't keep anything down. The doctor says to go to the hospital after four days of not eating or drinking. I.V.s begin. One at first, then every other day. I can't leave the house. I start disability from work. As I lie on the cold pink bathroom tiles for hour after hour, I think, "If only I had a dog bed to lie on."

I arrive at the doctor's office with a pink trash pail, complete with lid and box of tissues. The receptionist takes one look at me and puts me in a room with a bed.

"I'm throwing up black!" I cry as I show him my bucket.

He sends me across the street to a specialist. I'm examined once again. Some long name is given to me. Words that mean nothing.

I'm losing weight. Lots of weight. The specialist sends me to the hospital for a midline catheter. No access. Nurse after nurse, I.V. nurse after I.V. nurse give it a try with no luck. Finally the head I.V. nurse uses an ultrasound to guide her. I'm now attached to another wet bag, yellow with vitamins. I'm assigned an at-home nurse and filled with fluids through a backpack with a battery.

Is it worth it? What is this life?

I'm so weak I cannot leave bed to shower. Kevin runs a bath and carries me in. The warm wet facecloth on my back feels soothing. What a good man I have.

I only leave the house to see the physician. The only people I see are Kevin's family and Kevin. I send everyone else away. I am just too ill to talk. Summer is gone as has most of autumn.

Trouble. Pain in my mid-line catheter. To the hospital we go again. Phlebitis. Out comes my only access, and I am admitted.

Scared, tired, weak, nauseous. Will it never end?

Then there's pain in my abdomen. No worries, I'm told. Things are changing.

Back at home a visitor brings me a round watermelon. I eat it all by myself. It's the first nutrition I've had in a very long time. I keep it down too. But the vomiting returns and keeps me homebound. Months pass.

A party for me at Kevin's mother's home. She warns me ahead so I am as prepared as I can be. It was nice to be social for a bit, but after twenty minutes I have to lie down. The guests join me in the bedroom, one at a time, for a visit.

Winter is upon us. I've lost thirty-five pounds. The doctor says he's never seen such a weight loss.

Pain. Pain again. But different this time. The end is near. I call Kevin at work. I'm rushed to the hospital. Pain and vomiting. "Stay in bed," they say.

At 10:35 P.M. on January 5th my beautiful daughter Allison was born. She was 7lbs, 5oz and very dehydrated at birth. My illness has ended. Hyperemisis gravadarum they called it. I was sick from conception through delivery. These were tough times on my body, mind, and soul, but the end result was definitely worth it.

NO RINSING

It was spring. The flowers were blooming, the green leaves were on the trees, and the woodland creatures had emerged from their dens. It was on a beautiful spring day that I received a call from my mother-in-law, Judy.

"Do you have any tomato juice?" she asked frantically.

Apparently her English Springer Spaniel dog, Shelby, had been sprayed by a skunk and was stinking up her house. Unfortunately for her, I did not have tomato juice. I immediately hung up the phone with her and called the vet. What do think they recommended to get rid of skunk stink? The answer surprised me. Vinegar and water douches.

I called Judy back with the news and off she went in her little brown compact car to the local mega-mart after tying Shelby outside. No need to stink up the house any more.

When she arrived, she purchased seventeen vinegar douches. Yes, seventeen. The girl at the cash register had a funny look on her face when Judy approached her with her purchase.

"They're for my dog," Judy insisted.

"Sure, for your dog," the cashier replied.

Upon arriving home, Shelby was doused with seven bottles, top to bottom, and then rinsed. You can imagine my surprise when Judy called me to say it hadn't worked and the dog still stunk. I called the vet again and the reply was a laugh. Don't rinse the dog after the application were the instructions.

Thankfully Judy still had plenty of the feminine hygiene product on hand, having purchased every one they had on the shelves.

Once again, Shelby was doused with the douches. This time no rinsing. Hurray! It worked!

A few hours later my dog Katie got away from me and stuck her nose in a hole in the ground. A skunk's den of course. I was lucky, however. It was just her nose that got sprayed. Thankfully, Judy had one extra bottle of the magic solution, so I borrowed one from her with the laughing promise to replace it.

The next day Judy called me again. "Shelby has been sprayed again!" she shrieked.

This time she went to the pharmacy to make her purchases. She bought every douche they had. She said the cashier asked her if she was okay while paying for her items, and she informed her it was for her dog. The employee just rolled her eyes and said, "Sure, for your dog!"

RING-RING

10 A.M. Ring-ring. The phone is ringing across the street at my mother-in-law's house. Ring-ring.

No one answers. I'll try later.

12 P.M. Still no answer. Maybe she's in the bathroom. I'll try later.

1 P.M. Ring-ring. Now I'm getting worried. My mother-in-law Judy and I speak at least three times a day. We keep an eye on each other. We are quite close, and she is unwell.

1:30. Still no answer. Maybe she went out with her friend. Although, usually she tells me if she has an appointment or plans. I hope she's okay.

2 P.M. Nothing. That's it! I'm walking over there to see what's happening.

I leave the house in a rush, briskly crossing the street and knocking on her door. Usually I just walk right in as the house is unlocked and I have a key if it's not. But on this occasion the lock was changed the day before and I don't have a key as of yet.

No answer at the door. I peek in the window. Lights on. No one at the table. I bang on the window. Nothing.

"Judy!" I scream as I pound on the metal door.

In one swift motion the door opens and a man is standing there. My mind is racing. No men should be here during the day. They're all at work. And this is not one of them!

I punch him in the face, pushing him with my free hand, all the while kicking his shins. I'm fighting for not only my life, but Judy's as well. I'm hitting him hard time after time.

"TJ!" he screams. The fog immediately lifts from my brain. I know this man. I stop hitting him.

It's our family friend Daryl, and I've just assaulted him!

"Oh, Sweetie!" I cry as I envelop him in my arms. "I'm so sorry! I wasn't expecting a man to answer. I'm so sorry!"

He laughs and says, "Just remind me to never surprise you again!"

All is forgiven.

Apparently Judy's phone was off the hook and Daryl had called her. When she didn't answer, being a paramedic, he did what I did; came over to check on her. However, she answered HIS knock. I gave Daryl a thrashing that day. He came out of it with quite a bruise and a good story.

A story he's never let me forget.

Ring-ring. Judy was okay.

I TOLD YOU SHE WAS TROUBLE!

Her name was Mary, and she was trouble. She had a heart of gold and would give you her last penny, but trouble seemed to find her.

Mary loved to travel. She spent most of her early life in Massachusetts where she lived, worked, married, became a young widow, cared for her ailing mother, raised her daughters, and helped raise her granddaughters. In her senior years she moved to California to live with her cousin. She travelled to Hawaii, Scandinavia, Germany, Canada, and Mexico among other places.

It was on one of these trips that Mary found herself in a casino in Las Vegas. Not much of a gambler, she and her cousin John's wife, Lillian, decided to take in a show.

Being handicapped from birth, Mary would always get great seats at whatever event she attended. On this occasion she was right down front. The seats were perfect. Except...Well, Mary just couldn't get comfortable. Each time she moved in her seat she would scream from pain coming from her groin.

"Ouch! Ow!" she would cry.

During the performance Lillian and Mary headed to find the restroom. One was found, and Mary ran into a stall as fast as her crutches allowed.

"Were those men?" she thought, beginning to panic. "Ouch!"

Her pain returned while in the stall. Men were in the ladies' room, she had to pee, find what this horrific pain was from, and get the hell out of there!!

Mary stripped her under garments down only to find the pad she was wearing was stuck to her crotch instead of to her panties. She had put the sticky part on upside down and the pain she was experiencing was the pulling of her hair from the pad. With one giant scream she ripped it off and replaced it with a fresh pad from her purse. The correct way this time.

Now, what do I do with this pad and how do I get out of here? she thought panicking.

She grabbed the pad, opened the stall door, walked by two men facing a wall, threw the pad in the trash can, and sprinted out of the restroom.

Outside the door was Lillian. She stood under a large sign that read "Men's Room." Lillian was crying with laughter much to Mary's horror. Just then, the two men exited the restroom and one of them turned to the other and said, "Since when does Vegas have coed bathrooms?"

On the plane ride home Mary got up from her seat to use the restroom. As I'm sure you know from experience, bathrooms on planes are quite small. Well, with Mary a pleasantly plump old gal and her crutches, it was quite cramped. Mary sat on the toilet and put her false teeth on the edge of the sink as she was going to wash them. When she arose from the throne her teeth got snagged on her sweater and fell into the blue water of the toilet.

"What do I do?" she asked herself. "I'm on a fixed income and new teeth cost $300." Realizing she must retrieve the teeth, she plunged her hand into the toilet thinking the entire time, What do I do if I get my hand stuck?

Her hand and her teeth were now indigo blue. She tried washing, but no matter how much she scrubbed her hand and teeth they weren't getting any better. She wrapped her teeth and her hand in tissue and got out of the bathroom. Convinced everyone in the aisle was looking at her mummy-like wrapped hand and her toothless mouth, she nodded at each passenger as she went by towards her seat.

She spoke to no one until it was time to get off the plane and, since she needed a wheelchair, she had to speak, embarrassing her more.

Mary was met at the gate by her cousin John and his son Jim. Mary was always very talkative and when in the car on the ride home she kept her responses to a minimum, John realized something was up and seeing her blue hand he teased her as he often did "So, did you go fishing in the commode? You know fish can't get that high." She then informed him that he was a little shit and raised her fist shaking it in rebuttal.

When Mary got home, she soaked her hand and teeth in vinegar to remove the color. It worked, but her cousin John wasn't going to let it end there. One night at dinner he said to Mary, "I love that shit-eating blue grin!" Later, when she was boarding a plane for another trip, he shouted to her to avoid the blueberries on the plane.

Trouble seemed to follow Mary throughout her life. Mary's cousin John and his brother Joe were always teasing her. From the time they were little, they loved to harass their older cousin, all in good fun.

In her younger days, Mary and her daughter would take the train from Boston to Newburyport on holidays. There they would visit with Mary's Aunt Laura and her cousins. It was Thanksgiving and, after the meal of turkey with all the fixings, Joe and John were to take Mary and her daughter to the train station. The boys had teased Mary continuously from the moment she had arrived, but just as they left the house they presented the two Bostonians with a large wrapped gift.

"It's to say sorry for all the trouble we've caused you today," John said.

"Don't open it until you get home," urged Joe.

Mary and her daughter got on the train with the enormous box all wrapped up with a big fancy bow on top. Whatever could it be? Mary's daughter wanted to open it on the train. It was a long ride home and a young girl needed a distraction. After much debate, they decided to open the gift.

Off came the bow and all the wrappings. And what did they find inside? All the bones from the turkey dinner. Each one had a little bow wrapped around it. There was a note that read, "We told you not to open it until you got home." When I asked Nana Mary, yes, Mary is my grandmother, what happened to the box, she said they picked up their belongings and left it on the train.

I told you she was trouble!

T.J. HERLIHY is an award-winning, classically-trained musician and  listed in the *Who's Who of Music*. She enjoys needlecraft, reading, and writing. T.J. lives with her husband and children on a small farm in New England.

A KNOW NOTHING

I like to say I made a career out of knowing nothing. It's amazing how high you can go, knowing nothing, and when you get to the top, you often see you are not alone up there. There are plenty of other unqualified people just like you at the highest ranks of every industry. Not knowing anything never stopped me – but had I known what I know now, I would have tried more things – failed more and not agonized – on my way to success.

As example, earlier in my life, after watching the nightly Weather Show on Channel 4, I blurted out to my then husband, "That Weather Guy is a *Stiff*! I can do better than that!"

He looked up, quickly dismissed me, and went back to reading. I was twenty-one, in my senior year of college, and about to graduate with a degree in elementary education. As a woman then, I was the second string, holding my place in the working world till my twenty-five-year old husband earned his degree and started *the real career*.

"Do we have anything for dinner?" he asked, picking up his briefcase and getting ready to leave for the psych class he was teaching.

I was still calling my mother ten states away from the Piggly Wiggly pay phone to ask if it was okay to break a thirty-bunch of bananas, so it was wishful thinking that he even asked.

Teaching had been the plan till the day I woke up with an idea from a dream. I was always dreaming things, and a lot of them actually happened, so I thought, *Why not? 'Beverly Post, Channel 4 Weather Girl.'* I couldn't be worse than *the Stiff.*

Questions I never asked myself were – how would that happen? Or how could a girl with a thick New York accent be Weather Girl in South Carolina? Or even – how could a girl who only passed science because my mother begged the teacher not to flunk me, read a weather map?

No, I just had the idea and drove to the station. Channel 4 was a large and imposing building, but it never occurred to me not to walk in, so I did. Inside was a wide green entryway with the Channel 4 logo prominently displayed on the wall.

People were sitting on chairs waiting – intently looking at their scripts. They looked at me and quickly decided I was '*a nobody*' and returned to what they were doing. No one was at the desk so I walked to a red door and opened it – oblivious to the fact this was *never* done. Now I was in an office with a larger desk and an empty blue chair. There was a gold plaque on the blotter as a holding place for the person who commanded the desk. It read, '*Don't even think about going past here!*'

No one was there so I moved to the door behind it and opened it. Now I was in a long hallway with door after closed door. The walls were lined with award plaques the station had won with photos of their TV personalities, including the *Stiff's.*

One door was partly open so I walked over and looked in. A heavy-set man with light brown hair and dark glasses sat in a chair smoking, watching something on a screen. He looked up, not sure who I was, then hit his desk with the palm of his hand and gruffly yelled, "What do *you* want?"

That's when I thought about running but stayed put. I was running in my head but my mouth said, "My name is Beverly Post. I want to be Weather Girl. The guy you have is a *Stiff!*"

He looked up and started laughing. He was laughing so hard his cheeks were red and his eyes were moist. Then he seemed to remember he never saw me before and yelled, "Who the hell let you in? Yeah, he's a stiff alright. Okay, show me what *you* can do."

I had no idea what that meant so I just stood there, hoping he was going to tell me.

He thought I was funny. "Come with me," he said, leading me to a room with weather set.

Several cameras were on; boom lights pointed in different directions. He nodded and two men set up what would be my screen test. A woman led me to a platform. She picked up a wood block, snapped it in place, and yelled, "Take One."

On the inside I was screaming, but on the outside, I stood my ground trying to look like I expected this and was ready. Then it hit me – I had *no idea* what I was doing. He asked me to stand directly in front of a large map of the states and to talk to camera one. *Where was that?*

Music came on; it was the weather song I heard every night. Then he yelled from the back of the room, "Give us the weather report."

"Ahh, okay," I said, taking in a big gulp of air. The camera started moving as I looked up at the map. *There are no state names on the map* – **No S-T-A-T-E-S!** – I yelled on the inside. I had no idea which state was which, so I just started talking. I made things up. "Over in Kentucky," I said, pointing to Tennessee, "they are having a terrible storm…"

When I was done he said, "You were great, kid, but I can't hire you because you don't know geography! You can read weather from a prompter, but you need geography! So forget it."

I was doomed. I wouldn't be Weather Girl. I would never have my picture in the hallway. As he led me out, I turned back to face him; by now I knew his name was Burt.

I said, "Burt, how about *Romper Room*? I graduate in three weeks with a BA in elementary ed…How about *Romper Room*?" I said it slowly so it would sink in, not realizing I was being loud.

He stopped for a second and totally surprised me by saying. "Okay, you're hired! Got a Sag card? Don't worry about it," he said, waving his hand as if he were waving away the card. "Three Thousand Dollars."

In 1968, when my weekly grocery budget was $14 and you could eat steak several times a week with that, it wasn't terrible, but it also wasn't the $5,000 I had been offered by Fort Jackson to teach fourth grade.

I didn't care. I wanted it. I wanted to be on TV.

That night I proudly told my husband. He looked at me like I had four heads. "I have two more years till my degree," he said. "We can't do that." He didn't offer to make do or add another teaching course to his schedule. He just said, "No". And I accepted that *no*. It wasn't that he was trying to stop me – it was just that's the way it was then.

That was a long time ago. Times have changed, and I have certainly changed. My career would take me to different countries and help launch several large media companies, but I didn't know that then. Maybe I would have been a TV Star had I done it anyway, but most women in the late '60s didn't think that way; that kind of thinking didn't come to me for another ten years or so.

What I've learned by living is to just *show up in my life.* Don't be afraid if you don't know anything. Just say *yes,* even if you have no clue, because it can lead you to places you never imagined, and, if you really want what you're after, you'll find a way to figure it out.

ORGY ANYONE?

You never know in life what's around the next corner, especially when you are young, trying new things, and just flying by the seat of your pants. In the '90s I was feeling my way in what is now a global spiritual tribe. I have always been psychic and strange things often happened, but growing up in a small town in upstate New York where no one ever talked about these things, I felt different and confused.

It wasn't until I moved to Boston that I realized there was a whole *spiritual tribe* out there searching for meaning and, within that tribe, different divisions of spiritually talented people – psychics, mediums (both physical and mental), trance experts, tarot readers, angelic realm experts, and that was just the beginning.

I found myself in strange places on my road to discovery and before I located the truly talented teachers I could learn from, I kissed a lot of *frauds and frogs*. One of the earliest I remember was one we called *Sushi Rabbi*. His real name was Dr. Grummet Sphincter. Al went with me as the meeting was in the city at night and I still hadn't learned how to use trains.

People came from all over to hear Dr. Sphincter. We climbed four flights in an old Brookline brownstone and opened the door to see a room full of Sphincter followers. Some sat cross-legged on the floor or on yoga pillows. The smell of incense was thick, and people were chatting about what brought them there.

Making an entrance, he appeared from behind a silk screen wearing what looked like rabbi robes and thanked us for coming. He raised his arms and everyone stood; music came over the speaker.

"*Heyyy, ayy ohh, ohh…*," it was the melody from 'You Make Me Want to Shout."

Everyone started singing, "*Heyyy, ayy ohh, ohh.*"

After a few minutes, someone shushed the room. Sphincter's eyes seemed to blur and his face started taking on a different look. It was not the face of the man who had just greeted us.

This was an older man with larger lips and a protruding nose. I looked at him again, staring so hard my husband nudged me.

What was happening here?

His torso gently swayed and then he stopped and looked out at us. This was a new being entirely. Sphincter's *spirit guide*, Odom, began speaking in a deep voice that was almost like a loud whisper. It was coming from Sphincter's mouth but seemed far away at the same time. "All you *Persons on the Earth plane – as is below; so is above. We here in the Summerland are here to guide you in your spiritual development.*"

Summerland, we discovered, was another name for *Afterlife.* He continued an inspiring lecture on love and healing. After what seemed like a few minutes but was actually an hour, he bid us goodbye and the real Sphincter returned.

I had never seen a physical trance medium before. If I could go back now and re-watch him, I would know if he were the real deal, as I have known several stellar physical mediums since then, but in 1992 this looked amazing to me.

You never know who will show up at these kinds of events, usually smart people with professional careers who would never talk about things like a Dr. Sphincter trance lecture. In fact, Sphincter himself was a podiatrist in his day job and, at the time, I was running a company, but no one would know that.

Sometimes along with the real spiritual seekers you saw some strange or unusual people find their way to these events, like one we met that night walking to our car. A tallish Asian guy walked past muttering to himself and then slowed down to get in pace with us. He seemed to be in his late twenties – dressed in a gray suit and matching silk tie – overdressed for an event you sat on pillows.

He started talking as we walked together. "Can you believe that?" he asked in stilted English. We didn't get to answer as he continued, "*He* thinks he can talk to dead people? Boy, what a phony; what a fishy story. He expects people to believe that?"

169

Then he startled us with, "He no talk to dead people. *I talk to dead people!*" he said, raising his tone on the "I." And then he split direction from us and walked away.

‡ ‡ ‡

Al is a great partner because he doesn't study this subject but he is supportive of my endeavor. Over the years I have gotten myself into some odd adventures and often he will come with me.

That same winter we found out from a local holistic magazine that a group of psychics were meeting in Taunton to sit in circle and discuss spirituality and what it means to be spiritual.

I called to get an address and some directions (in those days Google was something you did if you were rude and staring too intently at someone).

It was a dark night on a country road and no street lights to see with. We drove up and down five times and never saw a house number. We were lost and late by the sixth time we drove by when we saw a brown, Cape-style house with red shutters. Someone was flicking the porch lights on-off; on-off.

"Oh, Thank God," I said as we pulled into the driveway.

A tall woman with long brunette hair fastened by small silver barrettes smiled sweetly as she opened the door.

Al said, "We thought we'd never find you."

The woman looked across the room to a young man standing near a hallway; she nodded and said, "Yeah, we know. We saw you drive up and down several times. I figured you were trying to find us."

"Thanks so much for looking out," I said.

The young man walked toward us and said, "No problem. Come on in, *you can take your clothes off* in the next room and join the others. "

My husband and I looked at each other and, at exactly the same time, mouthed, "*Holy Sh*t!*"

We could see a door at the end of the hall with eight pairs of shoes neatly placed together. The door was slightly ajar but dimly lit inside.

There were sounds coming from the room, but it was definitely not conversation.

We looked at each other, grabbed our coats, and quickly said our goodbyes, explaining we thought this was a Spiritual event.

Eventually we found the right house – *no flickering lights*. We sometimes wonder what we missed that night at the house we left in such a hurry.

ORGY anyone?

PINK JAIL CELL FOR ONE, PLEASE

One of the last things I remember thinking as I was being led out by gunpoint from a bank in 1982 in Rumford, Rhode Island was, '*Don't they know I used to be vice president of Hadassah?*'

I always saw myself as a do-gooder, but when I was thirty-four I ended up on the wrong end of the law, not even understanding why a gun was being pointed at me.

Still smarting from my divorce, I needed to find a way to support myself. A friend suggested sales, something at the time we both considered a low-level skillset – "*Anybody can do* it," she said.

Little did I know selling would actually be a huge career for me with mountains to climb – *and fall off of* – and peaks I never knew I would reach, but that would be several years later.

After scouring the hefty Sunday jobs section in the Boston Globe, I found several jobs but didn't think I was qualified to get any of them. Then I saw it: a position for a premium sportswear company selling to business owners. I had no idea what that was, but I did love clothes so I thought I might be qualified. I called and was told to go to their Providence office the next morning to interview.

Owning only three outfits I thought presentable for an interview, I chose a beige summer suit and added a pair of black patent-leather heels. I teased & sprayed my hair – *don't judge, it was the '80s* – and was ready to go.

As I pulled up to Unit 54 in an industrial complex, I saw a crowd of at least forty *twenty-somethings* standing outside waiting for the doorman like it was Studio 54, and I went to the end of the line.

Another young woman stood in front of me. She was statuesque, with deep auburn, shoulder-length hair, and the kind of beauty men always turned around for. Shewas the sort of woman other women worried about until she spoke to you. She went in the door before me and came out as I was going in. Smiling, she gave me a small wink as if to say, "You got this."

Two young men led me into a starkly furnished office with a long table covered with running suits stacked in piles and clothing racks on wheels all over the floor. I sat down, and Pete, the district manager, explained that the job would be selling sport clothing to companies as premium gifts for new clients. He explained a larger company might buy fifty or a hundred, a retail store might buy five. That was it; I was hired in fifteen minutes and told my training would be on-the-job with Victor, my manager.

Monday morning I met Victor in Providence. He was a large man with dark brown hair tied tightly with a rubber band. I got into his van and we drove to Rumford. After two hours of walking around in the hot sun wheeling a clothing rack full of sportswear, Victor was in a crappy mood. He seemed like a man who had already spent too much time doing things he hated. He said, "Let's go into that bank and you do the talking."

I guessed this was my first test.

Victor stood behind me as I knocked on the door to the president's office. A woman opened the door and said, "Mr. Tuscan is busy and not interested."

I almost left when a thought came to me and I went with it. "Please tell Mr. Tuscan we can help him increase savings accounts 20% if he will just give us ten minutes to explain."

She went to the president's office and came back minutes later with the defeated look of a woman always in charge who just found out she really wasn't.

"Meet him at the lobby desk," she said.

The bank was full of people at 11 A.M. Large windows streamed bright morning light into the lobby, and lines were already forming into the ropes off area leading to the tellers' counters.

The president walked through the lobby and sat at his desk. It looked like it had been made for pygmies – he loomed over it. He had a weather-beaten face that said too many golf outings and his nose had a smear of rosacea from his nostrils to the sides of his cheeks. His eyes were clear blue, his smile wide with teeth that were mostly white. You could tell he was a man who liked people. This was good for me as I clearly wanted to be liked and make my first sale.

I explained how our premium sportswear could be offered to bank clients who opened substantial new savings accounts and that the bank would get outstanding discounts for larger purchases. After twenty minutes he smiled at me and said, "Let's try it, little lady."

I pulled out my contract just as Victor decided it was time to get involved. He started telling the banker all the things he 'could contractually *not* do' in a testy voice, the kind that sounds like grating across a dirty chalkboard.

The president protested and Victor jumped up, hovering over his face. I tried to intervene when Victor called the banker a schmuck – not just any kind of schmuck, but a *stupid schmuck*. I took a deep breath and knew I was out of my element – what I didn't know was Mr. Tuscan had pressed a small buzzer under his desk.

Victor started talking louder now and people in the bank stopped what they were doing to look. Two officers walked over and, in a low voice, the stockier one firmly asked us to leave. Victor said he'd leave when he was ready. I bit my lip and looked down at the floor. *Should I tell them I am the past vice president of Hadassah?* I pictured the morning paper with my photo in it. A second later, I had something else to think about.

Both officers drew their guns. The larger one, in a voice that scared me, said sharply, "Get up and walk out."

I could feel the gun close to me. People were staring. We were cuffed and put in the back of a patrol car, me a little more gently than Victor.

"Where are we going?" I asked.

No answer.

Twenty minutes later, we were in jail. After taking off the handcuffs, they led us in separate directions. I never saw Victor again and can't say that made me sad.

They led me to a pink cell with a toilet.

Pink.

I sat on my cot and started to cry. With only one phone call and no lawyer, I decided to call Al, my boyfriend of six months. To his credit he took it in stride. The last time I'd called him my car was in a tree, so he was quickly getting accustomed to strange things happening to me.

Twelve hours later they let me out of my pink cell with no explanation why. I never went to jail again, and I never went back to that job, but it wouldn't be the last time I was led out at gunpoint.

ROANOKE

When you live in a world where the inside of your life is as big or bigger than the outside, sometimes they blend together, sometimes they crash. Either way, no two days are the same, and sleeping becomes the middle zone.

The morning light feels like a bang to my head. I hear the coffeemaker perking and Lucy, our beagle, whimpering, excited to fetch the morning paper. Lucy loves her job and never wants it to end, as evidenced by today's torn front page.

On the nightstand sit notes scribbled during the night. Reminders of things to do, remnant words or phrases heard in my night dreams from dead people (past and future), spirit guides who popped in, or up. Often what seemed logical at night made no sense in the day. Dutifully writing what I remember, I date the entry – Saturday, June 22nd, 1985 – Roanoke.

I am excited for the weekend ahead. We drop Lucy at the kennel and we're on our way. As my husband Al pulls onto Rte. 24 from Brockton, where we live, I hear 'ROANOKE' in my head – loud, like you were hearing it in caps.

"Al, I said, I hear 'Roanoke'." *It's great to have someone you love be your witness.*

Thirty minutes later I *see* the letters floating in my mind's eye. "Al, I see it again. What do you think it means?"

Neither of us has a clue – we are going to Cape Cod, not Virginia.

We get to the town of Yarmouth, our destination, and follow directions to the hundred-year-old inn where we'd be staying. Al is humming a song and drives right past. Realizing he's missed it, he takes his next left, pulling into the first driveway to turn around, and does a three-point turn.

In front of us at the top of the drive is a white SUV. The vanity license plate facing us has the word '**ROANOKE**' written in caps. We are exactly where we were meant to be in the universe at this moment. We look at each other and smile; this is going to be a great weekend.

THE BENEFACTRESS

When she walked in a room, she brought 1945 with her even though the rest of the world was in 1962. She loved the '40s and she wasn't going to give them up. Why should she? *That was your problem, if you let Time decide.*

I loved my Aunt Grace, but I never understood just how unique she was then. At thirteen I was aware she was *different*, but I loved that about her. When I knew her, she was already in her late fifties; tall for a woman – 5'11" – with long legs always enclosed in stockings that were thickish – clear, but somehow also a little hazy, like the kind women wore in wartime to save nylon. Her legs seemed to be fully planted when she stood up, and I wondered how she did that wearing three-inch platform heels – usually bright cherry red. I pictured her in a canteen during the war, dancing the night away with my Uncle Saul – her in the red shoes and him, wearing his Army sergeant's uniform.

Aunt Gracie was a big presence in my life even though I only saw her a few times a year. She lived in New York City with my Uncle Saul. They came with the other three brothers and their wives in a car caravan to visit my dad, the baby of the family, and my grandparents who lived nearby.

I loved the way she dressed. She had managed to keep all her 1940's bright-colored dresses in wonderful shape. She wore chunky plastic jewelry and dazzling red lipstick. Her arms were always exposed to show off her collection because, as she often told me, "a woman's arm is a lovely thing; be sure to wax yours weekly."

I had no idea what that meant. The only wax I was aware of was usually in a bucket and painstakingly applied to our kitchen floor by my mother on her knees.

Gracie's hair was as fascinating as her personality; a wacky shade of red that perfectly matched the rest of her ensemble and changed as often. Her features were thick for a woman but never seemed to detract from her appeal. Uncle Saul loved her and treated her like the queen she *knew* she was.

Saul was 6'3", a solid man who always left a big impression; well-built with curling silver hair that sometimes spilled over onto his ears. He was always dressed impeccably in the same gray-flannel striped suit and matching fedora. He loved his cigars and he especially loved his Scotch. I never saw him without a cigar, and I rarely saw them together unless they were enjoying their Scotch. They drank all day long but never seemed to get drunk.

My mother disapproved of the brothers and their wives because they either drank or smoked or both. Only the baby, my father, hardly ever drank; but he smoked and did other things that got him into trouble, like the time my mother grudgingly told me he'd had a contract put out on him and I had to follow him every night for a month in the summer of '67 to make sure he got home.

As I got older, we seemed to see Saul & Grace less and less. My mother said she stopped keeping the good Scotch since they drank whatever was free when they came to visit. I think she probably dismissed the thought that they finally figured out she didn't like them.

My father loved all his brothers and looked up to them. He loved to hear them tell stories about coming over on the boat to Ellis Island. Dad was the only brother born in America.

When I was seventeen we got a phone call from Saul. My father said Saul was distraught, "at his wit's end."

Saul had just spent three hours on the phone talking to people about Aunt Gracie. They were older now, but Saul still adored her and one of her best qualities was that she would *give someone the shirt off her back* if they needed it. Grace was a lover of people but sometimes she went too far.

So you can imagine his dismay when the phone rang and one of New York City's top-line charities called to thank them for the *ten thousand dollar* donation she had made in his name.

"What? Ten thousand dollars?" he'd wailed. "I am so sorry. Gracie meant well, but that check is no good. Please destroy it."

He hung up the phone, lowered his face in his hands, shaking his head – *that was the third call this month* – then he went back to watching his favorite TV show, *Bonanza*. There was little point in explaining to Gracie for the hundredth time that *he wasn't made of money*.

Instead he bent down and kissed her lightly on the forehead. She looked up, touching his face, and continued knitting hats for the homeless.

Hopefully we won't be one of them, he thought to himself.

HAIR SCARE

Breaking up with a hairdresser has never easy been for me. After writing my 'Dear Macy' letter over a week ago, I am still deciding between text or email. Anything that has to do with my hair is traumatic for me; for example the time I went bald for a year. Or the time I was leaving for my freshman year at college and a hairdresser permed and burned the hair off the top of my head. No one knows how mortifying it is to wear a cheap wig to college and have to sneak in and out of the girls' shower room with a turban.

When you've been seeing the same stylist for several years, it's just like breaking up with a boyfriend – you are out of circulation with no idea how to find a new one – but knowing in your heart, it's over.

I decided to check online reviews. Yelp doesn't always make it easy for people to give a review. I know, because when I tried to support a new Thai restaurant in my neighborhood, I ended up with my photo in the noodle section.

Eventually I found Flora. There were no photos of her work, so I had no idea what age range her clients were or what they considered wonderful. I called and in minutes got a text: *"Hi, this is Flora. I have received your call – if you would like to set up an appointment, let me know what you'd like to do and include a recent picture of your hair and a picture of your inspo. Can't wait to see you in my chair!"*

Wow, no one had ever done that; this was impressive. I took a photo of myself in the kitchen, in my robe, and texted it over. Your stylist is like your Mother Confessor, so all is well, even a photo with no makeup and wearing an old robe. I texted her some inspo photos of hair I didn't actually have but wanted, and we scheduled for two P.M. that day.

Flora's salon was in the back of a shopping center. I walked into what seemed like an endless hallway of doors leading to closet-sized rooms of single ownership hair, nail, and makeup salons. I had no idea something like this even existed.

Reaching her doorway, I looked in and froze. My eyes squinted tightly, and I took a breath trying to decide if I should *run*. In the next room stood my new stylist wearing a black and white dress with witches' faces. She had on high black patent-leather boots and across her forehead were five artfully placed black studs. Her glasses were turquoise, her hair bright red, and her bangs cut short. She looked at me and smiled.

'*Oh, my God,*' I thought. '*What do I do?*' Still planning my escape, I would say, '*Sorry. I walked into the wrong room*' and never give her my name; maybe she'd think I never came.

But of course I couldn't do that. My adult life had always been about following where Spirit led me, trusting I was in the right place, for the right reason. I looked up, and said, "Hi Flora, I'm Bev. Thanks for seeing me today."

She shook my hand and said how happy she was to see me. Her voice was gentle. Reaching up, she ran her hands thru my hair, like an artist choosing which pigments to use.

Then I saw the tattoo with skull and crossbones under her collarbone; in Italian script font it read, 'Beauty is Pain.' My hands clenched as I folded myself slowly into her chair.

She told me she considered herself a hair *artiste*, not a stylist, and that she was passionate about styling hair. I took a deep breath as the scissors started moving across my head. I saw my hair dropping to the floor. Flora told me about her life as a twenty-nine-year-old single mother of two trying to build her business and provide for her children. She told me about her passion for making things beautiful.

Getting a new stylist was a hair-raising experience, but the result was great – she gave me a wonderful cut. I wasn't quite sure I liked the notches she carved into the letter 'A' on the nape of my neck, but overall the cut was great. I was ready to send my 'Dear Macy' letter, ready for the breakup. I had found my new hairdresser.

BEVERLY POST has been a teacher, business owner, stand-up comedian, psychic medium, intuitive tarot card reader, newspaper columnist, and VP of Sales at three large media companies. She is a singer in a women's acapella group and loves to hike in the woods with her husband and dog where they live in the Boston area.

ALPHABETICAL INDEX BY AUTHOR